NEXT STOP—FORT LARAMIE

A Historical Novel

Frances B. Thorn

This is a work of fiction. Any resemblance of any of the characters
to persons living or dead is strictly coincidental.

FIRST EDITION

UNIVERSITY EDITIONS, Inc.
59 Oak Lane, Spring Valley
Huntington, West Virginia 25704

Dedication

I dedicate this book to my loving father, a native pioneer of Utah, who always encouraged me to further my education and go on to preserve our heritage.

Introduction

This is a historical novel about a courageous young woman Caroline Meade who leaves her comfortable home in New York to travel out to the wilds of the west to be with her husband, Peter. He is stationed at Fort Laramie, Wyoming Territory with the United States Army. She has heard how desolate these far flung army posts were but had no idea just how difficult the life would be until she arrived there by stage coach in August, 1850. There were only a few white women there. One was the wife of a sergeant, one the sutler's wife and five laundresses and seamstresses who were mostly foreign born and worked for the army. How she coped with the strange new life and adapted to the conditions there is the main theme of this book. At this fort Indians of various, tribes, mostly Sioux, mountain men, traveling emigrants, gold seekers and missionaries made the life there one of constant change and drama.

Contents

Chapter 1	Caroline and Peter............................	5
Chapter 2	Let No Man Put Asunder................	17
Chapter 3	Peter Goes to Fort Laramie.............	30
Chapter 4A	Caroline Travels West.......................	47
Chapter 4B	Caroline Arrives at the Fort............	55
Chapter 5	Life at Fort Laramie........................	74
Chapter 6	Council at Horse Creek...................	93
Chapter 7	Tragedy for Lieutenant Grattan.....	105
Chapter 8	The Harney Expedition...................	117
Chapter 9	A Year Goes By..............................	130
Chapter 10	Goodbye to Fort Laramie................	139

Chapter 3   Conflict Inside........................

Chapter 4   To Be Read in Silence................

Chapter 5   Crisis Goes to Port Louise..........

Chapter 6   Another Traveler......................

Chapter 7   Catastrophe at Sea, 1854...........

Chapter 8   Harbor Entrance......................

Chapter 9   Coming to the Crisis................

Chapter 10   Emergence Again and Escape....... 101

Chapter 11   The Heat of Coalition............... 111

Chapter 12   A Vast Class Life....................

Chapter 13   Tech Turns to Pacif.................

Chapter 1

Caroline and Peter

Caroline Meade stared at her image in her mother's gilt framed mirror hanging over the mantlepiece. She saw a small girl with a mass of dark, slightly curly, long hair which had been arranged in braids around her head and pinned in a bun at the back. Wisps of curls strayed out from her hair and softened the severity of her coiffure. A touch of corn starch had corrected the shine on her nose. She had a naturally rosy tint to her cheeks and her dark velvety brown eyes sparkled with excitement.

"Mama," she called. "Come and hear the list of things I will need on my trip to Fort Laramie."

Her mother who was wiping her hands after preparing a berry pie for supper came into the parlor. She hated to see Caroline go so far away from home but had stifled her disappointment for she admired Peter and thought that all young couples should be together if they could. She had learned from her friend Mrs. Parsons that her sister had gone out west. She had written her about her frightening experiences with the Indians and wild animals and the numerous hardships of living there.

She earnestly questioned, "Caroline, do you know all the difficulties you will have in traveling out there and living at such a desolate post?"

"Oh, Mama," Caroline answered. "I miss Peter so much I can't bear to be separated any longer and he wants me to come. I will be all right. I am sturdy and strong. Remember that Narcissa Whitman and Eliza Spalding went clear to Oregon with their husbands and Eliza was frail and ill."

"But you will be alone on the trip. Aren't you afraid?" her mother asked.

Caroline's mother was now sixty years old. Her gray hair was drawn severely back into a tight bun which made her normally pleasant countenance seem severe. Her calico dress was one which she had made in New England style. It had flounces and ruffles. It was made from material from her husband's store. He had a small general merchandise store dealing in general goods and dry goods. Caroline's two brothers Jed and Harry were married now. They had two children each. Caroline was very fond of Helen and Margret their wives and her nieces and nephews Susan and Carol and young Jed and Harry. It would be a difficult thing to say goodbye to them. Her brothers worked with her father in the store and their ideas for improving the stock and trying new merchandising methods had helped to make it into a successful business.

"Here is a pamphlet," said Caroline, "Telling just what

5

women need on the Overland Trail. Papa can get me anything he doesn't have now."

"I'm sure he will," said her mother. "But he is going to miss you so much. You know you are the apple of his eye."

"But mama, Peter hopes to soon be sent to a new post and I can go with him now he is a Second Lieutenant. It won't be a long assignment. I'm hoping he will soon come east so we can see all of you and he can get to visit his father again."

"Let's see what you need. You make a list and I will give it to your father tomorrow. It is only a week until you are to leave," her mother replied.

Caroline quoted from the pamphlet as she wrote out her list, "Female boots to wade through the mud, coarse needles, thread, yarn and combs. The clothing should be carried in a light trunk instead of sacks. There should be plenty of blankets, coarse towels, two good English merino or linsey dresses, three or four dark colored wrappers, two tweed sacks in place of shawls, one good silk hood, two sun bonnets, two pairs of buckskin gloves for the alkali dust is hard on your hands."

"I have most of the things and Helen will make me some sunbonnets. She is a fine seamstress. I will write down the things I don't have," Caroline said.

Her mother went back to the kitchen to finish cooking supper and after making the list Caroline went upstairs to her bedroom to see what clothes she could take and what things she would have to leave at home.

Caroline saw Peter's picture on her dresser and picked it up and kissed it lovingly. How handsome he was in his uniform. She sat down on the patchwork quilt on her bed. Her mind raced back to her first meeting with Peter. Her cousin Charles had brought him down to his home one weekend in June a year ago and she had met him at a dance in the churchhouse down the street. Charles, anxious to entertain his friend and introduce him to several girls had approached Caroline as she stood chatting with Helen near the entrance. She looked beautiful in her new dress made from a pattern she had drawn. Her dark hair framed a well-shaped face, her dark brown eyes sparkled. She had pinched her cheeks to a rosy glow and dusted her face with the new pink powder that her father had just added to his stock at the store. Her brown skirt flared becomingly below a white blouse trimmed with lace and ruffles.

"Caroline," Charles said. "I want you to meet my friend from West Point, Peter Meade. He ranks highest in our class. He will be a general someday."

Caroline looked into the deep blue eyes of Peter Meade. His dark hair was brushed until it shone, his uniform was well pressed and his boots spit polished. He was taller than Caroline who was only about five feet four inches. He was about five feet nine but not awkwardly tall. His facial features were well coordinated in a tanned countenance. Some magic attraction made them instantly aware that this was not a casual meeting but the beginning of a lasting romantic tie.

"How do you do, Miss Rushton," Peter said formally. "Your cousin has been talking about you. Would you care to dance? They are starting a square dance. Charles are you going to do the do si do?"

Charles hurried to ask Betsy Parkin, his girlfriend, to dance and soon the couples were dancing to the commands of the caller who was Henry, Caroline's brother. Peter was a good dancer Caroline saw and he admired the way she moved through the steps. When they came together briefly she took his hand firmly and smiled brightly at him. What a delightful girl, he thought, as she responded to the other dancers in a friendly way. This is going to be a good weekend. He already had been welcomed by Charles' parents and younger brothers who had made him feel at home in their modest but comfortable frame home.

When the dance was over Henry announced, "Refreshments will be served outside."

Charles and Betsy led the way to a long table filled with good food that had been prepared by the women in Reverend Tuttle's congregation. Several large trees provided welcome shade for the group and small wooden benches were arranged at convenient spots around the grounds.

Charles and Peter filled plates with the fried chicken, potato salad, rolls and punch and brought them back to Betsy and Caroline. They then returned to get some for themselves.

Betsy was a thin, prim and proper girl, attractive in a colorless way but lacking in vivacity and humor. She said to Caroline as they looked at their plates, "My they must think we have big appetites. I can't eat half of this."

Caroline replied, "That's just like boys. They can eat you out of house and home. I remember when Jed and Harry were home. I'll eat what I can, they were very gentlemanly to get it for us."

Charles winked at Peter as they filled two plates again, "Well, my friend, how do you like my cousin?"

"She's lovely," Peter answered. "I've never believed in love at first sight before."

"I want to see her again before we go back to the Point," Peter asserted.

"Where do you think you will go when you graduate?" Charles asked.

Peter paused and said, "I don't think I know. President Polk is pushing for people to go west to California and Oregon and they need army posts there to protect the emigrants from the Indians. It would be my luck to be assigned to Fort Platte or Fort Laramie. I hear that they are two of the most desolate and boring

7

posts out west."

"Well," Charles said, "You can be sure the army brass will pull some rank on us privates."

"Let's go back to the girls and enjoy today," Peter said. "Tomorrow will take care of itself."

Charles sat down beside Betsy. "Bets," he said, "I've known you since we were children and I've never noticed how blue you're eyes are. That blue dress you're wearing really brings out the color of your eyes."

"Oh Charles," she blushed. "You flatter me."

Peter sat down beside Caroline and balanced his well-filled plate on his knees. A faint odor of rose perfume made him aware of her presence. She was eating daintily of her salad and he felt suddenly very comfortable as though he had known her as long as Charles had known Betsy.

She said, "Don't we have some fine cooks in our neighborhood? They always have a good picnic. Mama made some of the potato salad."

"It's great," Peter replied, "And fried chicken is my favorite."

They ate quickly exchanging bits of information about their families and friends.

"My dad wanted me to go into the army," Peter said. "My grandfather was a colonel in General Harney's command in the Everglades. He fought the Seminoles in Florida."

"How exciting," Caroline said. "Do you know where you will be assigned?"

"No," Peter said, "But I hope it will not be out west."

Betsy was picking at her lunch. Charles said, "Bets, you're so thin, you just eat like a sparrow."

Caroline finished her plate and as Charles said, "Let's go down by the pond. It's just a nice walk. I need the exercise. Come on Bets." He took her hand as she rather reluctantly accompanied him. She was not an athletic type of girl and preferred quieter games and pursuits.

Charles said, "Peter can get to know Caroline if we leave them alone. Peter is a great guy. He will be one of the brass someday. He will be commissioned a second lieutenant when he graduates." He sighed, "I'll never be anything but a private or a sergeant."

"Oh Charles," Betsy said. "Don't run yourself down. You have done very well. Your friend seems to really like Caroline. Oh dear," she complained, "I just pulled the heel on my shoe. Please help me Charles, there's a grassy spot down by the pond."

She hopped along and Charles assisted her to a spot of grass under a willow tree by the pond.

Peter took their plates back to the picnic table and scraped the scraps on them into a barrel at the side and came back to

8

Caroline.

"Thank you," she said. "You're real handy. Let's walk down and see where Charles and Betsy went."

"My father and I have had to take care of ourselves since my mother died," Peter told Caroline. "I've had to clean up and wash a lot of dishes."

"My mother would love you," Caroline said. "Washing dishes is not one of her favorite tasks."

"I'd like to meet your family," Peter said.

"How long are you going to be visiting Charles?" she queried. "Could you come to supper Friday night? My folks would like to meet you."

"That would be fine," he answered. "I'd be delighted to come."

He took her hand and guided her to a path down to the pond. Charles and Betsy were talking earnestly and Peter said, "Let's go over to the grass under the tree on the right. I'm sure Charley and Betsy don't mind if we don't join them."

They walked over to the spot and Peter took off his coat and laid it down so she would not get grass stains on her pretty dress.

"Thank you," she said. "You're a real gentleman."

"And you're a beautiful girl," he replied.

"Tell me all about you," she said. "I want to know everything I can. I wish I had always known you."

"Name," he said. "Peter Marshal Meade, age 26, born in New Hampshire, raised in upstate New York, father and mother, Mr. and Mrs. Roger Meade. Mother died when I was nine. I am an only child so Father and I were good pals after Mother died of pneumonia. I am single and looking for the right girl." He looked into her shining dark brown eyes. "Now tell me about you," he pleaded.

"I'm Caroline Rushton," she replied, smiling at him.

"And you have two beautiful velvety brown eyes," he said.

"My parents are John and Evelyn Rushton," she continued. "My father owns a dry goods store on Fulton Street. I'm 20 and single."

He put his arm around her and she rested her head back against his shoulder. "Could I kiss you?" he asked.

"I have never kissed anyone when I first met them!" she answered, "And only once at fifteen when Jimmy a school friend stole a kiss, but I do know I have a special feeling for you."

"I'll wait," he said. "I knew you were a very special girl the moment I saw you."

"There's Charles and Betsy," she said. "They're ready to go home."

Reluctantly he helped her up and she smoothed her wrinkled skirt. He squeezed her hand as they parted and said, "I'll see you Friday. It will seem like years until then. We graduate at the end of the month and if I can I will come home with Charles again. I can't let you get away from me to some other fellow that might come along."

"Don't worry," she said as she reciprocated his handclasp. "I am really glad to have met you. I'll tell Charles to bring you again."

When she got home she took off her new ruffled basque and skirt and hung them neatly in the closet. Then she loosened the tight laces in the stays of her corselette and flung herself down on the bed to go over in her mind the events of the day. Wasn't he handsome in his uniform she thought. How considerate and kind he was. She pictured again his face close to hers, his deep blue eyes, dark hair, a warm male fragrance, charisma, not love yet but a growing infatuation that only needed some encouragement and experience to become love. She wondered if he had thought her a prude because she would not kiss him today. I hope not, she told herself. He will know that I am not a cheap, heartless hussy. But she imagined just how it would be to be kissed by him. She squirmed with delight and was aroused by her mother's call from downstairs. "Caroline, come and set the table, your father will soon be home and Henry and Margaret and the boys are coming to supper. Hurry, dear, you have been gone all afternoon."

She kept to herself her thoughts of Peter and went down to answer calmly all her mother's questions about him and their afternoon together.

"Did you like Charlie's friend?" her mother asked.

Caroline replied. "He's very nice. Is it all right if I asked him to supper Friday night? He would like to meet you and Papa."

"Of course," her mother agreed. "I'll get your father to get a nice rolled roast at the butchers."

"Thank you mama," she said, kissing her mother on the cheek. "You will really like him."

"Is Charles coming too?" her mother asked.

"No, he is going to see Betsy's new school where she will teach next year," Caroline replied.

"Are they getting serious?" her mother asked.

"Well I know Charles is," Caroline answered. "Betsy would like to teach a year before she gets married. Charles is afraid she will want to become just a school marm."

"She will be a good one," her mother said. "She loves children and has many good ideas about reading, writing and 'rithmetic."

"I hope Papa can use me in the store now school is over." Caroline said. "I'll want to be of some use and not spend the summer just loafing."

"I'm sure he'll find enough for you to do," her mother

10

answered. "I want to make several quilts, one for Helen and Margaret and one for you. I am going to put a quilt on the frames next week. Maybe Helen and Margaret and Betsy and her mother and Mrs. Carson down the block would like to come. We could have a quilting party. That would be fun and we would soon get it quilted."

Caroline's thoughts had gone back to Peter and the dance today. He had fit in with the crowd and enjoyed the day. It would seem a long time until Friday. She would have to plan for a special dinner and everything must be just right. The roses were starting to bloom now and she could arrange a lovely bouquet for the table. The American Beauties were colorful in their dark pink bloom and their fragrance was delightful.

"Caroline," her mother scolded, "You haven't heard a word I said. You must really be taken with that new boy."

"Oh Mama," Caroline blushed. "I've only seen him once."

Henry and Margaret came in just then by the back door and Henry said teasingly to Caroline, "Sis, you were really doing the do si do with your new beau. He's quite a handsome chap."

Margaret was getting larger now with her third child who was due in October. She was a hard-working, talkative, efficient housewife and a good mother. Her first remarks were addressed to the boys Jed and Harry who were heading for the big apple tree in the back yard. Between its branches was an old tree house built by Henry and Jed many years ago. It was in the state of delapidation, its paint gone, boards loosening and rotting and the ladder up to it missing some rungs. "Boys, be careful. You have your good pants on." They had all been to the church social and Margaret had stayed to clean up after the party. She had fried several of the chickens for the picnic. She sank down on a kitchen chair as Henry kissed his mother. She said, "Caroline, I do like your new beau. He's very nice and good looking too."

Caroline blushed. "I've only seen him once, but he is coming to supper Friday."

"He's in the army, I see," Henry said. "When will he be assigned to a post?"

Caroline said, "He's graduating as a second lieutenant at the end of the month. Charles was very complimentary about his army career."

"Well, old Charles should know," replied Henry. "He's been to the point himself."

Caroline's father, John Rushton, a graying man of sixty-four years came in just then. His face was lined from years of hard work and he was slightly bent from years of lifting heavy cartons.

"Margaret, how are you dear?" he said. "I saw the boys in the tree house."

He was very fond of both of his daughters-in-law and felt

his boys had done very well for themselves.

"Fine Papa Rushton," Margaret replied, "But I will be glad when this little baby gets here. The hottest months are ahead. I can't wait for a girl."

"We are all hoping that this time it will be a girl," Caroline's mother said. "Come now and call the boys, Papa. Supper is ready."

Jed and Harry came down from the tree house and Jed caught his pants on a protruding nail in the ladder and ripped them. He was crying loudly as he entered the door. "Jed," his mother scolded. "It always has to happen to you. Let's look at it."

Caroline examined the tear first. "Luckily," she said, "It's in the seam and it can be easily fixed."

"Good," said Margaret. "I'm tired tonight."

They enjoyed the supper for Caroline's mother was an excellent cook. After they had left Caroline went upstairs to bed and to recall the events of the day.

Peter had come here at 6 o'clock on Friday. Again as Caroline met him at the door she was impressed by his appearance and bearing.

"Hello," she said. "Come in and make yourself at home."

He removed his army cap and she hung it on the hall tree. He was pleased with the neat comfortable appearance of the parlor. The furniture was well-worn but polished. Its mahogany and oak exterior shone. On the walls were several large paintings of elderly couples and the mantle shelf had smaller pictures of young families.

"Are those your grandparents?" he asked.

"Yes," Caroline replied. "This is Grandpa and Grandma Barker, Mama's folks."

"They are distinguished looking," he said.

The pictures were taken in an unsmiling severe pose but they must have been good folks, he thought, to have someone as nice as Caroline for a granddaughter.

She looked lovely in the soft glow of the lights. Her dress was a bright blue and white calico with lace and ruffles down the front. Her dark brown hair was coiled around her head. Her large expressive brown eyes glowed with interest and excitement. She had pinned an American Beauty rose in her dark hair and this added to her attractiveness.

"Come and sit down on the sofa and I will show you my other relatives," Caroline suggested. "Mama will soon have supper ready. She took a big heavy black picture album from under the big oak table and showed him the other members of the family. They heard the arrival of Caroline's father from his store. He often worked late getting out special orders for his customers and arranging merchandise.

He came into the parlor and Peter was aware of the sharp, intent and direct appraisal of him by the older man. "How are you?" Mr. Rushton asked. "Welcome to our home. Caroline you go out and help your mother for a few minutes. She needs to have you mash the potatoes and get the things on the table."

"Papa," Caroline said. "This is Peter Meade, Charlie's friend from the Point. Please make him feel at home."

Caroline excused herself and went into the kitchen as her father and Peter sat down. She was thinking, I hope Papa likes him. He had always been very particular as to whom she had gone with and once said, "If he isn't a proper beau I'll chase him down the street."

"Did you and Charles start at West Point the same year?" he asked Peter.

"Yes, Sir," said Peter. "We met the first year and have been classmates all through."

"Good experience for a young man," Caroline's father said. "Charles was kind of a harum scarum boy but West Point has made him into a real man."

"Do you know where you will be assigned?" Mr. Rushton asked.

"Not yet but I hope not out west to the new posts. Colonel Harris just got back from out there and he had some very discouraging news about them. The Indians are beginning to resent the new settlers and are showing hostility to the emigrants."

"I agree with President Polk that we need to expand into the northwest and California but it is dangerous country. Only the French traders and mountain men have learned to get along with the Indians," the older man said.

Just then Henry and Margaret came in accompanied by Jed and Harry who were full of youthful enthusiasm. Caroline brought in her mother and introduced her to Peter. Henry and Margaret had met him at the social so they exchanged hellos.

"Come on now," Mrs. Rushton said. "Supper is ready. Papa sit at the head of the table, Margaret and Henry, Jed and Harry in your usual places, Caroline, you and Peter can sit here by me. I have to be on this side handy to the kitchen."

Jed gave Harry a cuff as they sat down, a brotherly attention that Harry seemed to resent.

"Jed be on your best behavior," Margaret instructed. "Be nice to your brother."

Caroline's father gave the blessing asking God to bless the family and the food prepared for them.

"Sis is a great cook too," said Henry. "Mama has taught her all she knows and Margaret has learned how to make her famous apple pie."

"Oh Henry," Caroline flushed. "You used to say I was a

little nuisance."

"When you followed Jed and I every time we went fishing down at the pond you cried when we put the worms on the hook."

They were a typical, loving family, Peter decided, teasing each other and bantering, yet revealing an underlying feeling of devotion to each other.

"Would you like another piece of strawberry shortcake?" Mrs. Rushton asked, as they finished their meal. "The berries are ripe in our patch now."

"No thank you," Peter said. "Everything was so good that I am full to the top."

Mrs. Rushton beamed and decided that Peter was a well-brought-up young man and that Charlie had good taste in friends.

They arose and Caroline said, "Would you like to see our garden. We have a swing out under the apple tree." Peter followed and they went out the back door and down the path through the orchard. Henry and the boys were throwing a ball back and forth. Margaret was helping her mother-in-law with the dishes. Mr. Rushton was rocking on the front porch and enjoying the evening breeze talking to neighbors and friends as they came along the sidewalk in front of the house.

Caroline spoke first as she and Peter seated themselves in the wooden swing, "Isn't it a lovely evening?"

"Beautiful," Peter said. "I enjoyed the supper and your family is so nice and friendly that I felt right at home."

"I love them," Caroline said. "Papa works so hard in the store. Henry and Jed have been a real help to him."

"I hate to leave you and go back to the Point," Peter said, "But I must graduate and get my commission. I have been working toward this goal and my father really is set on seeing me finish. Charlie has invited me back when we are through and I hope to see you then."

Her beautiful brown eyes were fastened on him and he suddenly felt very close to her. He put his arm around her and she rested her head on his shoulder. The fragrance of June roses filled the garden and made him slightly giddy. He bent quickly and softly kissed her on the mouth. She responded and suddenly their lips touched ardently and he was delighted at the sweet softness of her skin.

"You're so lovely," he said. "I hate to let you go. I have been looking for a girl like you all my life."

"You are such a gentleman," she said, "And tender and loving too."

"We have to be tough at the Point," he said. "We are taught all the skills of battle and defending our country. Some of the men are rough and the little niceties of most people are forgotten sometimes. Out in the field conditions are primitive and especially when fighting Indians in the west. My great-grandfather fought at Concord and Valley Forge."

"Mine too," said Caroline, "And my great grandmother Hazel was allowed to go there in the winter to be with him. He was an officer in the army and several log cabins were built to house them. Martha Washington came from Virginia to be with the President."

"He was a great man and only think what we would be like now if we were still a colony of Britain. Sometimes men have to take a stand and the women must be there behind them."

"Let's forget all the problems," Caroline said, "And just enjoy being together. Are you and Charlie leaving in the morning?"

"Yes, very early so I must say goodbye to you when I leave tonight but for just a little while."

"I will be waiting," she said, "And good luck on your graduation from West Point."

"Thank you," he said. "This occasion has been one of the most special of my life."

They sat just holding each other for a long time, listening to the birds singing in the trees and the mournful cry of a loon on the pond, then he kissed her once more and they felt a sudden burst of emotion that made them tremble.

"Let's go back," she said. "Henry and Margaret will be leaving to get the boys home to bed and we want to say goodbye to them."

The light was fading in the west, dusk was settling down blotting out the garden and the trees and nearby houses but still the fragrance of roses filled the air and he hesitated to leave her.

She took his hand and held it tightly as they walked back to the barn yard.

"Oh, you're back," Henry teased as Margaret shooed Jed and Harry back into the buggy. A large black horse was pawing the ground, wanting to leave the hitching post and get on home. Henry took the reins, slapped Blackie on the back and they were off, waving to his parents and Caroline and Peter.

Mr. and Mrs. Rushton and Caroline and Peter went inside and Peter said, "I must be off too. Thanks so much for the delicious dinner, Mrs. Rushton. It was nice to meet you sir," to Mr. Rushton.

"Come again," the older couple said.

"I will, you can be sure," he said earnestly.

Caroline's father put his arm around his wife and they went back into the house.

"Caroline," Peter said. "I like them very much."

"I'm glad," she said, "And glad that Charles brought you here. Please come again."

"In a month," he promised, and quickly kissed her on the lips. "I hate to go," he said, "But I have to."

"Goodbye," she whispered and watched until he had disappeared up the street in the dark.

Chapter 2

Let No Man Put Asunder

Peter had been on leave for a short time after graduating from West Point and before being assigned to a post as a second lieutenant. He had come home with Charles then had renewed his courtship of Caroline.

In the weeks that followed their love for each other had only grown stronger in their closer association. She had all the qualities he wanted in a wife and she saw in him the realization of her girlish dreams. They decided to be married in the middle of September before he had to go home to receive his army orders. They agreed to be married in her mother's home by Reverend Tuttle. He had written to his father that he had found the girl he wanted to marry and that he was sure his father would love her too. He promised to be home in August to attend to things at home and then be down to Charlie's a week before the ceremony. They had chosen the 12th of September for the wedding and he wanted his father to come down and stay at the Rushton's. Her father and mother had invited him to stay at their home for they had Harry and Jed's spare room upstairs for guests. He was sure that his father would be most welcome and the Rushton's wanted him to come. They planned to spend three days on the beach on Long Island if they could stay in the cottage that George Simmons owned and then would accompany his father back to Albany to stay until Peter knew where he was being sent and if Caroline could accompany him.

Peter had come on the 7th of September as he had promised and they had spent every possible moment together. The Rushton house was the scene of much confusion as Caroline's mother and sister-in-law and brothers rushed about getting their house clean and neat, the wedding dresses made, the food prepared for the guests, and the many tasks it required for a home wedding. On the 12th Peter had taken her with him to meet the train on which his father had come.

"Father," he said as an elderly thin man came down the steps with his bag, "I want you to meet the lovely girl I am going to marry."

Caroline looked up into two blue eyes that were so like Peter's and felt the warmth of the older man's firm handclasp.

"My dear, I am so glad he has found a girl like you. From what he has written me I am sure you will be a great help-mate and wife for my son."

"Come," she had answered as Peter took his bag. "My Ma and Pa want you to stay at our home. We have an extra room all ready for you."

On the way over in the buggy Peter and Caroline had

chatted and his father had enjoyed the ride. Caroline's father and mother had welcomed him warmly and Peter and Caroline had shown him to his room upstairs.

Caroline said, "You can freshen up in the bathroom off the hall. We will be downstairs. Everything is in confusion for we only have two days before the big day. We hope you feel at home."

"I'm sure I will. Your family is so warm and friendly," he had answered.

Hand in hand Peter and Caroline had run down the stairs.

The pungent odor of chrysanthemums had filled the house. The huge bouquets of red, purple, and white flowers filled vases and were banked beside the mantlepiece before which they would say their vows.

"You must be going," Caroline said to Peter. "Charles is having a party for you men tonight and I must have Margaret and Helen and Betsy try on their Bridesmaid's dresses to be sure they fit right. Margaret and Helen have done all the sewing and are dears to help us."

He kissed her now quite firmly on her waiting lips.

"Sweet dreams tonight, dear. Day after tomorrow you will be mine." he said.

Caroline's father had called to him as he went out of the hall. "Peter could I have just a minute of your time? I would like to talk to you."

He faced the older man. He suddenly felt very immature and shaky as he realized the seriousness of a life's commitment.

"You will be good to Caroline?" her father asked. "She is a very special girl. Her mother and I want her to be happy. You will be a kind husband to her and I will never be sorry I gave her to you." It was as much of a statement of his feeling as a question. He had appraised Peter and had accepted him into the family but a loving feeling between daughter and father had made him want to be sure.

"I will always love her as I do today," Peter spoke up quickly. "I will never cause you to regret that I married her."

"Then we will be happy to have you in the family," Caroline's father said and patted Peter on the shoulder.

Peter had left with all the conflicting emotions a prospective bridegroom has. He was waiting for his orders to a new post in the army hoping that it would be in the east where he and Caroline could make a home near their parents. He had seen how his father had aged since he had been at the point. He had looked frail and not too well when he and Caroline had met him at the train depot.

After a few days at the beach at Long Island he would take his father and Caroline home to upstate New York where he could show her the scenes of his childhood and the beautiful

Adirondack and Catskill mountains. He was glad that her folks had welcomed his father so warmly and was sure they would soon be good friends. Both fathers had a similar background and should find much in common.

He had remembered the sweet warmth of Caroline's lips and the softness of her skin. He had hurried faster up the street to Charlie's house.

Caroline had spent the evening hours in a whirl of prenuptial arrangements. Betsy had come and stayed an hour trying on her salmon colored bridesmaid's dress and seeing Caroline's beautiful white satin and lace bridal gown.

"Oh," she screamed delightedly in quite unusual exuberance for such a quiet girl. "You will look so beautiful in that dress. How do you feel tonight so near to the wedding? You will only be a single girl one more night."

Caroline could not organize her feeling now. So much emotion had gone into the last few weeks that she had suddenly felt weak and shaky.

"Oh Betsy," she cried. "You will only know when you and Charlie set the date and get married."

"I am teaching now at the old school," Betsy answered, "And Charlie doesn't know where he will be sent. Maybe next year we will decide to take the plunge depending on where Charlie is," Betsy answered.

"Don't put off too long," Caroline said. "Charlie is a dear steady boy and needs someone like you to push him a little. He would make a good husband."

"I love the colors we're wearing," Betsy said. "They go well with the autumn flowers and the colors of the chrysanthemums."

Caroline went down the hall to see if Peter's father was rested after his trip and found that his door was open and he had gone downstairs to visit with her parents. Her mother was making the last preparations for food for the guests at the wedding and Mr. Rushton and Peter's father were sitting on the setee in the parlor exchanging views on politics, religion, and telling family stories. They had found they had many general views about life and experiences to exchange. Their families had much in common and both fathers were pleased with the choice their children had made.

"Caroline is a lovely girl," Peter's father said. "I knew that when he brought her to meet me. Peter is waiting for his orders to a new post and I am hoping to have him assigned near us but with the moving of Mormons west to the Great Salt Lake Valley and the settling of California and Oregon the army needs soldiers to man posts along the way to protect the emigrants on the trail. We can only hope that things work out for them."

"Her mother and I am hoping that Peter will be assigned to the east but now since the Mexican War has ended and the

Treaty of Guadalupe Hidalgo signed there are many easterners wishing to go west to settle the new territory and there has been a call in Congress for forts along the trail west and the need of officers from West Point to lead them."

"Colonel Stephen Kearney made an expedition west two years ago to try to impress the Indians with the army's firepower but I am not sure how it did effect them or if it did any good," said Mr. Rushton.

"We will be happy to have you stay with us a few days while Peter and Caroline honeymoon on Long Island," said Mr. Rushton.

"He does not have a long leave," Peter's father said, "and they must be back up home by September 20th to receive his orders. He wants to show Caroline our home and interesting sights around it before then."

"Come and meet my sons and daughters-in-law," her father said. "My wife and all of them are very busy today. I am very happy with my sons' choices. Margaret and Helen are fine wives and my four grandchildren are live little crickets. My sons help me in my store on Fulton Street."

They went into the kitchen where Margaret and Helen were busy putting the finishing touches on the three-layered wedding cake, and Harry and Jed were helping their wives in any way they could. The four children were outside swinging and playing ball.

"Come and meet Peter's father," the elder Mr. Rushton said. "He is staying with us while Peter and Caroline are honeymooning."

Helen was wiping a bit of frosting from her fingers and Margaret stopped adjusting the bell on the top of the cake to greet their guest.

Peter's father saw two pleasant looking dark-haired young women, one who was quite obviously pregnant and both neat and attractive.

"We are finishing the cake," Margaret in an obvious statement said, "but we are happy you could come down to be here at Peter and Caroline's wedding. Please make yourself at home. Ma and Pa Rushton are glad to have you come."

They shook hands and Harry and Jed dropped what they had been doing and came to shake hands too.

"Good to see you sir. We are happy to have Peter in our family." They were sturdy young men with a slight resemblance to Caroline and the same dark eyes.

"I am happy to be here with such nice folks," Mr. Meade said.

"Come on out into the yard," Mr. Rushton invited. "We have had a good garden and although it is September the chrysanthemums are blooming now and the trees are turning into their beautiful fall colors. Where is Ma?" he asked his daughters-in-law.

"She went upstairs to make the last adjustment on Caroline's dress," Helen said. "I must finish this cake and help her."

"Please excuse the last minute confusion," Mr. Rushton said. "There is so much to do for the wedding. Let's see the garden."

The two older men had gone out and after showing him the garden area they had seated themselves on a wooden bench to get the warmth of the September sun. "September is such a lovely month," Mr. Meade said. "If this good weather could only last."

The day of Peter and Caroline's wedding the 12th dawned bright and lovely. Everyone was up early and Caroline in a daze of prenuptial emotions had brought Peter's father down to breakfast which her mother had hurriedly prepared. She was too excited to eat and only nibbled at the food.

First Margaret and Helen came to assist Caroline and Harry and Jed dressed in their best dark suits and leading the children and cautioning them to be on their best behavior and not to get into mischief or soil their clothes.

Peter's father went upstairs to change his clothes and rest awhile before the ceremony. He had not been too well and he spoke to the picture of Peter's mother he had placed on the dresser. "Dear, I am sure you would like Caroline and her folks who are quality people. I'm sure you would be happy to see Peter marry such a lovely girl."

This mid-September day was one of those beautiful days of warm sunshine and colorful orange and gold hours that are a prelude to the cold stark winter scene. Caroline's mother and her sister-in-law had been preparing for several weeks for the occasion and had pressed through a thin cotton cloth the purple grape juice for the punch for the guests. Charlie would slyly add some gin to it to provide a sparkle. Mrs. Rushton and Helen and Margaret had aged the rich dark fruitcake and cut thin slices to seal in tissue paper as a gift to the guests to put under their pillows at night. The house shone from general cleaning and polishing, Grandpa and Grandma Rushton seemed to be almost smiling from their usual serious poses from their pictures above the mantlepiece.

Caroline in a flurry of excitement had laced up her corselette and had it tied by Helen to cinch in her waist to the smallest dimensions. She put on her lace trimmed panties and her chemise and underskirts and then Margaret assisted her into her beautiful bridal dress. She had curled the ends of her dark brown hair slightly with a heated curling iron and it fell in a cascade around her shoulders accenting her sparkling dark brown eyes.

She pinched her cheeks, put a light powder on her nose and said to Betsy who was putting on her bridesmaid dress.

"Well, how do I look?"

"Lovely," they all said. "What a beautiful bride."

Mrs. Rushton came in then and helped Betsy fasten her dress. "Betsy," she said. "You look lovely too."

The bright color had transformed Betsy. She usually wore drab black and gray clothes.

"Caroline," she said to her daughter. "We have talked before about being a good wife and mother. I feel that you and Peter love each other but with Peter's uncertainty about his future I must give you a little advice now. Be patient and understanding, never jump to conclusions and always end the day with good will. Everyone must make compromises in life there is no smooth and easy road."

"Ma," Caroline said. "You and Pa have been an example for me. I shan't forget what you have taught me." She kissed and hugged her mother and then they all went downstairs except for Caroline who waited for her father to take her down the stairs.

Mr. Rushton was happy for the bridal pair and came in wearing his best black suit, a chrysanthemum in his button hole.

"Come," he said. "They are all here. Peter and Charlie and Reverend Tuttle. I am giving you away but dear I hope you both will always remember that this will be your home if you need one and you will always be welcome."

"Thank you, Pa," she said. "You have always been so good to me."

They walked down the stairs to the wedding march played by Mrs. Tuttle on the organ and Caroline saw Peter in his army dress uniform, his dark hair gleaming, straight and erect in his bearing. She walked forward and met him at the wedding altar. The others, Harry, Jed, her mother, Margaret, and Helen were only a blur. They were part of the small crowd who had come to see the ceremony.

She was conscious of only part of Reverend Tuttle's ceremony and advice, "Dearly beloved, we are gathered here together to join in matrimony these two young people." She had answered "I do" and heard Peter's firm answer to the Reverend's question and then his advice and warning, "Whom God has joined let no man put asunder."

Reverend Tuttle had come early to see if he could help in any way. He had seen Caroline grow from a shy toothless six year old to the lovely young lady she was today. He had talked to Peter and Caroline when they had come to see him at the parsonage one evening to tell him of their plans and ask him to marry them.

He had seen the love in their eyes as they had come to him. There was no mistaking their devotion. He had advised them about the need for always being honest with each other and never holding a grudge overnight. He had told them too that marriage was too sacred an obligation to take lightly. He had seen many instances where the marriage vows had been broken and the unhappy consequences for the couples. He had prayed last night that this union would not be like many others. He knew Peter could be called away by the army and that only by strength and love could they endure the separation.

Then Peter had pushed the ring on her finger which Charlie had fumbled for in his pocket and kissed her ardently.

Everyone rushed about them offering congratulations and best wishes. Family, friends, and neighbors were there. Mrs. Rushton asked them to cut the wedding cake and Peter took the big knife and handed it to Caroline. She cut the cake and then Mrs. Rushton invited everyone into the dining room to enjoy the refreshments. Little Jed and Sally passed out the tissue wrapped pieces of the wedding cake as the guests left.

Caroline kissed her mother and said goodbye to her sister-in-law and brothers. Harry was taking them to the Long Island Railroad in the surrey which they would take to reach their destination a little cottage on Hempstead Bay. It was owned by a friend of Mr. Meade's another professor at the college.

Peter had brought his suitcase from Charlie's and he said goodbye to his father and told him they would be back in a few days to go home with him to Albany.

They had all enjoyed a piece of the wedding cake and the friends and relatives had left and Caroline had gone upstairs to change into her going away suit. It was a brown alpaca with a ruffled blouse with a lace front that Helen had made. She came down with her bag which Jed took and carried to the buggy.

He said to her as he passed, "Sis that was a lovely wedding. Have a great honeymoon."

She remembered the time when she was only their little sister, an unwelcome tag-along, to her brothers in their more adventurous exploits. Now she was a married woman and their roles had changed. She kissed him on the cheek and thanked him for helping with the wedding.

Harry did most of the talking while they were going to the train. Telling them of the interesting things that had happened to he and Margaret when they had been married. Peter and Caroline held tightly to each other's hand and only wanted to be alone together.

Peter took Caroline by the hand and helped her onto the train and Harry handed them their bags. "Goodbye Mrs. Meade," he said. "Be seeing you in a few days. Enjoy your visit to the bay."

She waved to him and called, "thank you Harry. It's nice to have a brother like you."

They were alone now and Peter put his arm around her as they rode along and she rested her head on his shoulder. Her brown bonnet, rimmed with a bright feather and braid was laid aside and he asked, "Are you tired dear? It was a great wedding. Your folks are wonderful but we didn't get much sleep last night. Charlie's party lasted until the wee hours."

"And I couldn't sleep. I was so excited," Caroline said. "How far do we have to go?"

"Only a short distance," Peter said. "George Simmon a friend of my father's from upstate and a professor has a summer cottage at Hempstead Bay. He has been there most of the summer and has left some food, wood, and blankets there for us. He is coming down next week to close it for the season. We are lucky to get it now."

"I brought my bathing suit," Caroline said. "It is a blue one with ruffles on the pantaloons and around the neck and a cap to match. Pa got it for me from a salesman in his store. I hope the water isn't too cold to swim."

"You will look beautiful," he said. "I can't wait until we get to the cottage. Rest your head on my shoulder. It will only be a short ride."

She answered, "I've never been to the seashore. It will be heaven to be there with you."

She laid her head against him and the rhythmic click of the car's wheels on the track made her sleepy. He looked down at her lovely face with her long dark lashes covering her brown eyes and marveled that he had found such a sweet vivacious girl. Her dark brown hair curled around her small delicate ears as her face reposed in sleep.

Such a feeling of complete satisfaction at their closeness came over him that he blushed to think of his desires. Tonight they would be fulfilled, but he must be tender and loving for she was a special girl.

The train came to the station near the bay and Peter gently awakened Caroline and he carried their bags as they left the train.

"Oh dear," she apologized, "I must have really been tired."

Peter whose right arm was slightly numb from holding her said, "It has been a busy two weeks and especially for you. Come dear, we can walk to the cottage. I have been here before with Father."

It was almost getting dusk as they found the cottage.

Peter opened the wooden door with a big key and set the bags down as he carried Caroline over the threshhold.

They fell onto a wooden bed with a lumpy mattress and lay there. He kissed her ardently and passionately and she responded eagerly.

"You are so lovely and so sweet," he said. "It has been hard for me to wait until we were alone. Coming up on the train was the longest trip of my life."

"I am yours for all time," she said the sounds of the water

on the shore and the squawks of seagulls finding food along the surf made no difference to them at all.

Much later Peter brought in their bags and locked the door.

"Tomorrow," he said, "I will show you the bay and most of the summer residents have gone home now so we can have the beach to ourselves."

He made a small fire in the old iron stove because the September nights were getting cool and the dampness of the ocean penetrated the wooden shell of the cabin.

"George was very good to leave us the food and firewood," he said.

Caroline got up reluctantly and said, "Are you hungry? I know from my brothers that men need good meals. I'm really not lazy dear."

"Let's forget about food for tonight. We can have a good breakfast for George and Ann have left a good larder here."

"You have been such a dear tender lover that I must tell you how much I appreciate it," she said. "It was a new experience for me. I was waiting just for you."

"Me too," he said. "I could never love another girl like I do you. I've had girl friends before but they could never hold a candle to you, Mrs. Meade."

"I love my new name," she responded, "but it will be a little while before I realize I'm not Caroline Rushton."

Morning came and they slept late reveling in their intimate knowledge of each other. Peter had held her in his arms with her long dark hair falling around her shoulders and framing her well-shaped face. A stray curl had fallen on her cheek and as she awoke and opened her big brown eyes she was aware that he was scrutinizing his new bride and that he was delighted with her.

"Peter," she said. "I'm going to get up and make you a big breakfast for I know you must be hungry now. Harry and Jed would be calling for food now and hurrying Ma to get their breakfast."

"I'll light the fire and make coffee," he said. "Father and I had to do for ourselves when mother died."

She put a wrapper over her nightgown and slippers and went to see just what food was in the cupboards.

"They left some eggs and bacon," she said, "and bread. I'll fry you some and toast some bread in this wire rack over the fire. Here's a jar of strawberry jam."

"Sounds good, Mrs. Meade," he said as he kissed her. "Especially since my darling is preparing it. After spending the years at the army mess at "the Point" this should be a great breakfast."

The awareness of her new role made her slightly nervous but Peter's obvious approval gave her confidence to proceed.

"I'll do better when I have more experience," she said. "Ma

is such a good cook that I haven't had to do too much cooking."

"Never mind," Peter said gallantly. "Here I'll get the toast before it burns."

"How do you like your eggs?" Caroline asked.

"Turned over and well-done," he said.

"I'll have mine sunny-side up," she said, "and not too firm. I'll take mine off first."

She removed her egg from the pan and let Peter's egg continue to cook.

"Could you cut some slices from this slab of bacon?" she asked.

He got a cutting board and a big knife and cut several thick slices from the meat.

They ate relishing the food and Peter said, "Darling after breakfast, we'll put on our bathing suits and wade out along the shore. It's beginning to get warmer for the September sun is nearer to the earth and hotter now."

"You know so many things," she said. "I can never learn all you have to teach me."

"It is an advantage to have a professor for a father," he admitted. "Father taught me a lot about astronomy and the planets."

Caroline still feeling shy and modest before Peter took off her wrapper and nightgown and put on her new blue bathing suit with its ruffled cap and pantaloons.

He had borrowed Charlie's bathing suit and it was slightly too big for his well-built muscled frame.

He laughed in good humor at his plight. "I forgot my suit in my haste to get back to you," he acknowledged. "Charlie was good enough to lend me his. He is rather more rotund than I am."

"You still look handsome to me," Caroline said.

"And you look so pretty with your hair tucked up under your cap and your beautiful brown eyes sparkling. I am such a lucky man even an oversized suit can't deter me a bit. Let's make the most of our few days and not think about the future."

They walked out to the beach, hand in hand, breathing the crisp salty air and scattering a flock of seagulls that were scavenging for bits of food washed up from the sea.

Caroline put a tentative toe into the water and found it was quite cool. Peter took a more aggressive step into deeper water and gasped as the cold surf rushed into the bay, then as he got used to the temperature he urged Caroline to join him.

"I'm not a great swimmer," Caroline said, "so I'll just dog paddle in the shallower water."

He swam out farther, breaking the water with smooth crawl strokes and then came back to her.

"There aren't many ships out there today," he said. "Most of the pleasure boats have been docked for the winter."

"You wonder where all the ships are going," Caroline said. "My great-grandfather came to Massachusetts from England in the early 1700's."

"Mine too," Peter said, "and my grandfather fought the British and finally the Seminoles in Florida. He was in the army too. I wish he were here today and then I could get a better assignment. He was a colonel."

They enjoyed their swim and then he said, "It is too cool to stay long in our wet suits. Let's go back to the cabin where we can get warm for a change." They saw only one other man far away up the beach and Peter said, "he's likely a guard left to patrol some cottage area. It's quite deserted this time of the year."

"Just you and I and our love and the sea and the cottage," she said. "We have no need of more."

He took her small, firm, tanned hand in his big rough one and they made wet tracks in the hard sand of the path, as they went back to the white frame cottage.

"I wish we could stay here forever," he said.

"Me too," she echoed. "It has been so delightful. I will remember it always."

"I could only hope that life could be as simple as it is today," he added. "I'd like to forget that I am still waiting for my orders to a new post but no more of that. I'll race you to the cottage."

She ran with her wet blue suit flapping around her but he caught her at the steps and held her and kissed her so passionately and long that she was trembling with emotion.

"The wind is cool," she shivered slightly, "Let's go inside."

The embers of wood in the little iron stove still kept the cottage comfortable and warm and the privacy of its rugged interior made a world just for the two of them.

Later they talked about their childhood, their families, their home, and their dreams of the future and discovered many new things about each other that they had never known before but nothing that made them less sure of the love for each other.

The last day of their honeymoon dawned cloudy and threatening. Peter said, "It looks as if it is going to rain. We must catch the train at four."

She stretched sleepily, completely satisfied and reveling in their shared feeling of happiness.

"Oh, Peter," she said. "I hate to go back. You have been trained and disciplined at the Point. My folks have always been so kind and gentle to me. I'm not lazy," she said spunkily, "but I have been protected by my parents and by my brothers. I have been sheltered and I guess I am naive as to the outside world."

"I'm glad you are sweet and unworldly," he responded. "I

will protect you always."

She felt the strong muscular force of his arms about her and she relaxed in complete joy.

They ate their breakfast late in the day and she prepared it singing gaily as she stirred the pancake batter and turned once in the big iron frying pan. Peter took the pan from her and said, "I am great at flipping these things." He expertly tossed the hotcake into the air and caught it as it turned.

"Smarty." Caroline said. "Give me time and I can do it too."

"Just something I learned when Father and I lived alone," he laughed.

They packed their bags and Peter left a note for George and Ann thanking them for the use of the cottage. Reluctantly he locked the door, deposited the key in a can by the steps and helped Caroline down to the path which led to the train station.

"I hope Father has enjoyed his stay with your folks," he said. "I have been worried about him. He hasn't been too well lately but he was very happy about our marriage."

"I really liked him," Caroline replied. "I'm sure we will be friends. He reminds me of my own Pa."

"They have many interests in common," Peter agreed. "Father has taught at Albany college and has many friends at school but he retired last year and he has been lonely with my mother gone and me away at the Point. He wanted me to have an army career since my grandfather was an officer. We have had army men in our family for a long time."

"And men of courage and discipline, I'm sure," Caroline answered.

They caught the train and watched as each mile passed wanting to make the most of each hour together knowing that an uncertain future lay ahead.

Harry met them at the train station and took them back to Caroline's house where everyone was waiting to greet the honeymooners.

In their quiet state of contentment they took their bags up to her room after greeting their parents. He hugged his father and said, "It was great at the bay, Father. George and Ann had left everything we needed. We will be leaving tomorrow for home."

His father looked tired but pleased after the hectic events of the last few days. They all sat down to a good dinner prepared by Caroline's mother and Jed asked, "Well newlyweds, how was your stay on the Island?"

"Wonderful," Caroline said. "It was a little cool at night but the first two days were gorgeous."

"I'll bet you didn't know how the weather was," Harry said.

Caroline blushed and reached for Peter's hand under the table.

"We stacked all the presents in Harry and Jed's room. Peter's father didn't mind the clutter. They will be here when you get settled," Margaret said. "Several came after you left. One from Aunt Harriet in Connecticut. She wishes you well."

"We must go up later and see the presents," Caroline said. "Shan't we Peter?"

He nodded and returned her query with a squeeze of her hand.

They spent the night in her bedroom and it seemed quite different here now with Peter beside her. All the years she had spent here as a child and a girl seemed to recede in her memory. She was a wife now and must adjust to all the new experiences that a shared life would entail. She wondered if she could possibly live up to his obvious opinion of her. For them life stretched in uncertain paths ahead but she went to sleep thinking they must meet one challenge at a time.

Chapter 3

Peter Goes to Fort Laramie

Peter had written Caroline from Fort Laramie to explain the situation there and farther west and the difficulties the emigrants were having with the Indians. They were beginning to resent the number of emigrants who were killing their buffalo and moving through and into their land. On May 18, 1845 a company of crack dragoons, the heavily armed cavalry, had left Fort Leavenworth and with them were three hundred men and officers. They had carbine pistols and sabres, two mountain howitzers and 12 lb. ball exploding shells, military rockets and fireworks. With them for food they had taken thirty head of cattle and sheep, a store of flour and eighteen barrels of salt pork and bacon. For more rations they had found buffalo plentiful and antelope and deer in the hills. They had traveled about twenty-one miles a day.

Peter wrote how this group under Colonel Stephen Kearney had passed some of the emigration of 1845 on the North Platte two days east of Fort Laramie. Colonel Kearney had sent a rider ahead to arrange a council with the Oglala Sioux. On their way they had seen a large village of Brule and Thomas Fitzpatrick the mountain man and explorer who had been their guide, had rode across the river to invite them to meet with Kearney. The braves dressed in fancy dress and decorated with bear claw necklaces and many scalps had come riding down the river to meet them. Colonel Kearney talked to them of peace and had showed them his weapons. The tall army horses had made the Indian ponies look small. The Brule were fearful of the white man's firepower and had trembled like aspens in the wind at the sight of the fireworks. For an example of their own courage and skill at riding and hunting they chased and killed an antelope. Their horsemanship was something that had made the soldiers marvel. Colonel Kearney had asked them to attend a council at Fort Laramie. The soldiers had been amazed the next day to awaken and find that the whole Brule village had disappeared.

Their expedition had arrived at Fort Laramie on the 15th and after the long, dusty, tedious trip the men were glad to be there. There Colonel Kearney had found the Oglala and Brules ready for a conference. The soldiers in dress parade uniform had ridden to the council which had been held on the flat ground between the old fort and the newer one. A frame of lodgepoles had been built by the Indians at the fort and had been covered with buffalo robes. Benches and chairs had been provided for the officers from Fort Platte. The Indians had hoisted three banners. The army responded by firing three rounds of the howitzers and then sending rockets to show their strength. The officers had seen that the Indians were terrified. Just then a wagon train had come and driven its wagons into a circle at Fort Laramie.

After impressing the Indians with the arms power, Colonel Kearney had taken his men to the Divide, had scouted along the Oregon Trail and then had returned to Fort Laramie. This expedition had not stilled for long the Indian's resentment and desire to get revenge against the intruders who were cutting scars across the landscape with their wagons, using precious grass and timber and killing many buffalo for sport or food. More and more of them were coming west now.

Later in 1847 the Mormons had begun their treks west and hundreds of their wagons followed the northern side of the Platte River and moved out over the Mormon Trail. The Mormons believed as Brigham Young said, "It is better to feed them than to fight them," but still the young braves had harassed the trains as the buffalo became more scarce and more and more emigrants came west.

A large band of Oglala and Brule camped at Fort Laramie and demanded food from every train that passed the fort. They became more and more insolent and were even snatching coffee cups which they were offered. They rode in escort of the trains moving west from Fort Laramie and followed them for miles. The chiefs tried to stop them but they did all the mischief they could.

The ill-fated Donner party of 1846 while passing the Sioux encampment at Fort Laramie had been accosted by fifty warriors trying to steal things and even snatching articles from the hands of the emigrants. One of the leaders had ridden to the Sioux camp and told the chief. The chief had ridden to the train and ordered the braves to return back to camp or be punished by the rest of the tribe.

The government soon found that the Kearney expedition had not stopped the problems on the trail. The United States government had created a new Indian Agency on the Upper Platte and had appointed Thomas Fitzpatrick the first agent in August, 1846. Knowing the Indians well from his travels through the region, he rode from village to village trying to allay their fears and to stop their depredations and horse stealing. By 1847 President Polk advocated that army posts be built but the Mexican War stopped for awhile this plan and all government resources were diverted to fight this war. Discovery of gold in California in 1848 at Sutter's Mill and the sudden onrush of emigrants west to California made it imperative to have army posts to protect the wagon trains. Peter wrote again to Caroline about the situation and that he was being transferred west to Fort Laramie.

The fur trading post at Fort Laramie had become an important stop along the trail. Here were discarded many outworn wagons, excess baggage and dead oxen. Many travelers sought to lighten their loads before reaching the mountains and threw obsolete and unnecessary goods away. Some decided the trip was too perilous and turned back at the American Fur Trading Post at Laramie but most kept on their journeys.

When the gold rush was at its height, troops were sent out from Fort Leavenworth to establish posts along the Oregon Trail at Laramie and on the Platte. Peter received his orders to move out with Brvt. Major Winslow F. Sanderson and to proceed west. He wrote to Caroline and said he was disappointed to be ordered west but there was a great need for the army to protect the trails. He had been hoping to be sent to an eastern post so Caroline could join him there. He wrote that he would not be writing again until he got to Fort Laramie for the trip was hard, through Indian territory and he would be unable to mail a letter unless they met some travelers who were going east. He would let her know just how conditions were there.

Peter was disappointed at his assignment but following army orders he left with the cavalry from Fort Leavenworth, in May, 1849. He had been given a big black gelding named Diamond for a mount. He was called that because of the white diamond on the front of his head. The stableman had saddled the horse and brought him around to the officer's quarters for Peter to see. Peter took an immediate fancy to the big horse and patted him on his head. He was a strong, well-built animal capable of making the long trip to Laramie. The horse nudged Peter's shoulder and whinnied.

"Will he do sir" the private asked. "It is a long journey west and Major Sanderson said it is important to have a good horse. Diamond is just that and he has a good temper too."

Peter looked at his new companion and decided that he was a fine horse. "Good old Diamond," he said, adjusted the bridle and again patting his head. "We have a hard journey to make together. Get him ready," he told the boy. "We are leaving tomorrow."

Peter arose early to follow his commanding officer Sanderson in riding out of the fort. Behind the officers and men were several howitzers and supply wagons and a herd of cattle and sheep. The animals were to be used for food on the trail. Barrels of flour, salt pork, and bacon were also taken along. The trip was over 2,000 miles and besides their supplies they could hunt for wild game and catch fish in the streams.

They proceeded down the dusty road and each day would bring new experiences. Peter was not happy to be going so far from Caroline although he respected Brvt. Colonel Sanderson and wanted to do his best to help him in this move to Fort Laramie. Caroline's letters had been irregular because of the mail service to Fort Leavenworth. Sometimes he had received five at once and then several weeks would go by without a word. He knew she was writing often and he replied just as soon as he could. The faint perfume on her stationery had given him a longing to see her and caress her again. The warmth and sweetness of her personality would always be with him. He was glad she was safe at home with her parents for now he was on a journey fraught with danger and unexpected consequences.

In September of 1848 the news of the gold find in California had appeared in the *Baltimore Sun*. From then on the news had spread in the east and had excited interest all over the United States. By January of 1849 thousands of men seeking to find riches in California were waiting on the Atlantic coast to sail around Cape Horn and travel through the jungles of Panama to get to the gold diggings. Equal numbers were traveling from the east to Missouri to join wagon trains heading for California. These were the travelers whom Peter would meet. Every type of person would heed the call of the west, doctors, lawyers, farmers, mechanics, politicians, and thieves. It was a motley section of humanity who searched for gold.

Many times on the trip Peter and his men would be called upon to help some stranded emigrant who had succumbed to the pressure of merchants in St. Joseph and overloaded his wagon. Starting out in May with plenty of grass for their stock they would later reach the plains in the dry season and lack food for their animals. It amazed Peter how many of them were ill-prepared for such a journey. Ill-cured bacon went green in a week, beans, crackers and flour got weevils and every imaginable kind of gimmick and patent medicine were included in their supplies. Shovels, bellows, and gold machines loaded down the wagons.

One wagon train had stopped at a small stream and Col. Sanderson's men decided to stop; on the opposite side for the night where a grassy spot would be good pasture for their stock.

As Peter dismounted he heard a small dark-haired girl call, "The soldiers are stopping for the night. Now we don't have to be afraid of the Indians."

Peter ordered his men to dismount and make camp. He went to a small shallow pool to wash his hands and face. The cool water felt good after a day's ride in the dust and noise of the trail. They had had to stop frequently to get around a long wagon train which was cutting several trails in the terrain of the prairie.

There seemed to be much confusion in the camp. Peter could hear loud angry male voices debating over the course they should take and the leadership of the train. This was a large train of about 21 Conestogo wagons with loads of over 2,000 lbs. One wagon had a big sign on the side, "California or Bust." The drivers were positioning their wagons in a circle as prescribed by knowledgeable travelers. The stock herders were driving the several hundred cattle onto a patch of grass up the stream. Many of the oxen were young and poorly trained for such a long journey. Some balked at being unhooked from the wagons while others ran off and the unhappy owner had to chase them and bring them back to the wagon. It was an anxious task for the herders who had to see that the cattle and horses had grass but must also keep a wary eye for Indians who if not openly hostile could steal part of the herd.

So far the Pawnees had kept far back from the army train. The scouts had seen them in the distance but the sight of the many mounted soldiers had made them draw back from their usual habit of accosting the emigrants and demanding gifts.

As evening came the camp quieted for awhile and the smell of baking bread and burning willow wood came drifting across the stream. Peter and the soldiers were fed beans and beef from the commissary wagon and had to line up with the officers first to be handed a tin plate and a cup of coffee by a civilian employee accompanying them. A pair of men crossed the stream on horseback and rode up to the army camp and addressing Peter said, "Lieutenant can we ask you to help in deciding just which one of us should lead this wagon train? We have been arguing all day and since Henry Harper the wagon master was buried a few miles back we don't know who to choose to lead the train."

"I'm afraid," said the older dark-haired man, "we're both pretty inexperienced at leading a group of people across such barren and rough country. We started out from St. Joe in good shape but when Henry took sick and died we were left with only a group of young farmers from Ohio who have never traveled west of the Mississippi. Most of the teamsters had never seen an Indian until we met some Pawnees back a few miles and we started out thinking it would be a lark to travel west and find a fortune of gold in California. They had never had to drive an oxen or mule and did not realize the dangers on the trail."

Peter said, "We are going to Fort Laramie. If you want to follow along behind us we can lead you on the right trail to get there. Colonel Sanderson is leading this group of soldiers and is a fine commander. We will be starting out at six in the morning if your wagon train can get ready to travel by then. We have had no Indian trouble since leaving Fort Leavenworth. They seem to be staying back from the trail and you should be safer traveling along with us."

"Fine," said the younger man. "We will tell the people to be ready to go at six. They were happy to see your soldiers arriving today. The women and children will be grateful for your help."

"Couldn't you divide your responsibilities and both help to lead the train," Peter suggested. "Here we have certain duties and each officer is doing his job."

34

"A good idea," the blond younger man said. "George, you can be the leader since you are older and I will be your assistant. There is room for both of us in directing this wagon train."

Later that night the sound of music came across the river and of people laughing and singing and dancing. A sergeant said to Peter, "They seem to be enjoying themselves, I wish I was back home with Sadie. We loved to go to the dances at the post." Peter remembered how Caroline had looked at their first meeting and he longed to see her once again.

But now he must tend to his duties and see that all the men were in bed so they would be ready to go when the bugle blew in the morning. He said, "Private, is our tent ready?" It sounds like our neighbors in the wagon train like to think that we are here to protect the trail."

"It makes you feel real good to know that we are able to help some," the young soldier answered.

The bugle awoke the sleeping soldiers as the sun was just breaking over the east and they saw that there were signs that the wagon train was getting ready to follow them. Men were yoking oxen to the wagons and driving them into a line ready to follow behind the army train as it pulled out of the camping spot along the trail. They would be eating the dust of the prairie as they traveled in this position but they would feel much safer than they had before their meeting.

In these years tens of thousands of ox teams would leave the Missouri outfitting stations and thousands of oxen would die on the trail. The California Trail would be known as the trail of the "mouldering ox" as many would be killed by thirst, alkali water, or Indian arrows. The Forty-Niners would not wait to bury their animals and the trail would be outlined with broken wagons and the skeletons of oxen, horses, and mules. Peter and the army expedition would see many such reminders of the difficulties experienced by the thousands of travelers who were going west in search of gold.

The Kearney expedition had been sent out to frighten the Indians and keep them in check but it had not succeeded in its purpose for the continual use of the Indian's land by the onrush of the white men could only bring further trouble.

Peter and his companions saw the chaos wrought by the emigrants as they proceeded west and wondered how long the Indians would allow this to happen without a serious incident. They had, however, been instructed to discipline the redmen and protect the emigrants in cases of incidents involving both on the trail. The government in Washington had decided to expand the country to the Pacific Ocean.

Travel along the Platte had been boring and dusty. The army train made its monotonous way by the river. Peter and the other soldiers were discouraged by the thirsty, shadeless trip and camped at night by the river. Only then could they refresh themselves and wash some of the dirt from their faces and hands. The string of islands with small amounts of wood could be reached only by riding into the shallow river.

"Hell must be something like this," one disgruntled sergeant said. "The hot sun of summer made my men feel like parched corn. Laramie will look good after this trip." He took his horse down to the stream for the animals were suffering too from the heat and dust. The commissary wagons had been held up for their wheels had to be tightened frequently because they were shrinking in the hot sun. The emigrant wagon train followed the soldiers meeting all the same inconveniences. From here on the fires would have to be made of buffalo chips for there would be no wood on the plains.

Other wagon trains had left their marks on the trail as many emigrants had died of cholera and had been buried there, some in hastily prepared graves.

Peter told Major Sanderson as they ate their evening meal, "The men are getting weary of the long days in the heat and dust. I'll be glad when we see Chimney Rock and the bluffs. They aren't too far from Laramie."

"Look," Peter told the supply sergeant. "There's a herd of buffalo up on the hill."

"I'll tell Major Sanderson," he replied. "He'll send some of the best marksmen out to get some buffalo meat. It would taste good now. We've been on dried beef and beans for several days now."

"It's no cinch to get one," Peter said. "The old bulls are apt to charge and gore your horse. They will have to place their shots carefully and then wait to be sure the buffalo is down. They can run a long ways with a ball in them if it isn't in a vital spot."

Major Sanderson had ordered a group of soldiers to pursue the herd and bring back some buffalo meat. The change in diet would help the men to forget the trials of the day.

The soldiers came back with enough buffalo meat to make the cooks work longer to satisfy the appetites of the men. Two young bulls an a cow had fallen to their muskets and they had soon been slaughtered and skinned and the meat prepared for roasting over the fires.

Peter's friend Sergeant Butler commented on the special treat of buffalo steaks and said, "As we get farther west, antelope, elk, deer, and fish will be available to improve our diets."

Peter said, "There is nothing better than a tender buffalo steak."

Tomorrow they could cross the Platte at the California crossing where many wagon trains crossed. Ahead was rolling, rugged country between the North and South Platte. Dry washed out gullies would be a challenge to the wagons causing damage to the tongues and axles. The wagon masters cursed as they had to negotiate the rough trail but the army train made its way slowly north over the highlands. It was a stiff climb for the expedition as they traveled up over the water-cut gullies and made the drop down Windlass Hill into Ash Hollow.

Peter riding along with the Sergeant had to pull back on Diamond's reins as the big black sure-footed horse slowly made his way down the rock trail. "Whoa boy," he cautioned, "this is a steep part of the trail."

He had to stop to help one teamster whose wagon had gotten away from him and had killed a mule and broken his own collar bone. He rode back to summon the doctor who was with them to help the teamster who had been caught under the wagon.

Ash Hollow was a pleasant stop after the day's trials on the dusty and rock trail. It was a lovely, wooded spot where many wagon trains paused for a few days to recoup their morale, wash clothes, and make repairs to their wagons. Here was good grass for the animals, water and firewood. Several wagon trains were camped here too as Peter saw as he rode into the area. The army train found a good spot to camp and the tents were soon up and the cooks were busy getting a meal ready for the soldiers.

A band of Sioux Indians were camped there too, their tepees arranged in a circle. Dressed in colorful headdresses and deerskin clothes they surveyed the oncoming army train and the howitzers and the chief and some warriors were loudly discussing the possible meaning of such an expedition into their lands. They were wary of the troops and did not make any attempt to associate with them. They were, however, begging at the emigrant's camps for sugar and tobacco and liquor.

Here at Ash Hollow were several graves. One gravestone showed that a girl named Rachel Pattison had died when only 18 years old. It was a grim reminder that tragedy as well as adventure was a part of the trail west.

The Court House and Chimney Rocks were interesting sights to break the monotony of the weeks of travel along the Platte. Rising above the landscape these unique rocky formations could be seen for miles ahead. The army train camped on the trail near Chimney Rock and some of the more adventurous soldiers made the long trek to see it and climb up above to look down on their camp about three miles away.

When they returned one private said, "It was farther than we thought. Man am I tired after that hike and climb."

Peter said, "Wash up, chow is ready. We're leaving early in the morning. Scott's Bluff is ahead."

Scott's Bluff, Peter learned, had been named for Hiram Scott an explorer and mountain man who had been left to die in the hills by his companion and had crawled many miles alone to perish here under the bluffs. The army expedition took the trail that made a side sweep away from the Platte by way of Robidoux Pass through the high clay cliffs. Here Robidoux with his Indian wife had built a stopping place with a blacksmith shop and store.

Peter halted his men and they dismounted and went inside to get a drink after their dusty, long ride. Now they were thirty-five miles east of Fort Laramie and Laramie Peak could be seen rising in the distance.

Peter said to Sergeant Butler as they entered the store, "Won't be too long now and we'll be at Fort Laramie. We should be there in two days if we can cross the North Platte without delay. I hope the ferry is not too busy."

Fort Laramie was the main stop along the trail here for refitting and resting before crossing South Pass and traveling into the Rocky Mountains so it had become an important post. Traders made money in selling goods at inflated prices to emigrants needing the necessities of life after the long trip over the prairies and plains. They were willing to sell unnecessary equipment at cut-rate prices, over-heavy furniture and household goods to lighten their loads. Many emigrants weary of western travel, ill, and lacking good oxen and equipment, turned back at Laramie. Others set up camp for the winter there and made a nuisance of themselves by destroying the surrounding countryside and carousing at the fort.

Peter and Major Sanderson had become good friends on the trip west and he relied heavily on his officers to keep the new recruits and non-commissioned officers in line and doing their job on the trail. Peter adhered strictly to army rules telling the men that they must keep a constant vigil to prevent an Indian attack or dangers from wild animals and to be alert to watch for buffalo and game which could add to their monotonous diet. Sanderson had won his Brevet rank by gallant and meritorious conduct in the Mexican War. He and Peter were both from New York, both had graduated from West Point so they had much in common. On July 17th he and his men trotted into Fort Laramie. They were to reconnoiter the surrounding countryside and see if this would be an advantageous site for an army post to protect the emigrants who were being harassed by the Indians.

After investigating the country north and west of the fort for a few days they returned and Major Sanderson gave the orders to purchase the fort from the American Fur Company.

Peter was glad to be settled at last after the strenuous trip from Fort Leavenworth and rode Diamond, his faithful horse into the stables. He had become attached to the big black horse. He had brought him safely across the rough country over streams and gullies without faltering or falling by avoiding prairie dog holes and taking a steady gait down treacherous rock trails. Peter patted Diamond on the head and told the private who took care of the horses to unsaddle him and give him a rub-down and then feed him some oats. Diamond whinnied as Peter strode away. Things were very unsettled at the fort with the fur company leaving and removing its possessions, the Indian tribes camping there wondering what was happening and trying to assess the new situations, and the new arrivals finding a place to stay and arranging for new owners at the fort.

Peter soon learned the history of the fort from listening to stories told in gatherings at the settler's store. In 1841 the American Fur Company had seen the need of a post here for buying furs and then it was called Fort William in honor of William Sublette who was a mountain man and one of the owners of the post.

One of the first occupants of the old fur trading post at Laramie was Caleb Bentwood, a typical mountain man. Peter saw him standing by the store as he and his men rode into the fort. As Peter dismounted he came forward to greet him.

"Hello, Lieutenant," he bellowed. "I'm Caleb Bentwood. I'm mighty glad to see you and your men. Injuns been causing trouble around here and on the trail. Hope you can settle them down. I have a Sioux wife, good woman too, keeps our lodge outside the fort neat and clean."

Peter saw that Caleb was just like the mountain men that had been described to him. His low-crowned wool hat covered a long unruly shock of graying hair but underneath twinkled his gray-blue eyes that were sharp and friendly. He was dressed in buckskin clothes that were fringed at the seams. His jacket reached to his knees and his trousers were tight wrinkled leggings. On his feet were moccasins made of deer skin. His skin was like leather and burnt to an almost Indian color by the exposure to sun and wind. A leather belt was around his waist which held his flintlock, pistols, his knife for scalping and skinning and his hatchet. A pouch flung over one shoulder held his bullets and over the other his powder horn. Attached to these were his bullet mold, ball screw, and over the other his powder horn. Hanging from these were his ball screw wiper and awl for leatherwork.

Peter replied cordially, "Good to see you Caleb. You can teach me some things about this part of the country, the mountains and the Indians. I'm a greenhorn out here."

"I'm going out for a few weeks to trap along the rivers nearby," Caleb said. "I'll be back right smartly. I'll be glad to do anything I can to help the situation. I got a feeling for both Injuns and whites. I hate to see them squabbling all the time. I figure there is a place for both in this big country. See ya when I get back."

With that Caleb went on to get his pinto Indian pony which

was tethered to a post in front of the store. As he went he rattled loudly as his accoutrements of metal and wood moved with him.

Just then a sergeant, newly stationed at the fort came to see if Peter knew his way around. He was a big red-haired young man with a florid face, bright blue eyes and a hearty handshake. "Hello," he said to Peter. "I'm Ned Delaney First Sergeant of the 2nd Division Infantry. I have only been here a short while. I came with Colonel Kearney's expedition but went back to Fort Leavenworth with him only to be sent back out here. My wife came out just a month ago. Welcome to Fort Laramie. There aren't many buildings here yet but with the army sending more men out they are planning on building new barracks and stables too, and a chapel and a hospital as soon as possible. One detachment has been sent to get limestone blocks up the Platte to make foundations for them."

Peter knew instantly that he had found a friend. He replied, "Ned, I'm glad to meet you. I'm Peter Meade, Second Lieutenant of Cavalry. Tell me all you know about the situation here."

"You must be tired after your trip and reconnoitering on the trail," Ned replied. "Why don't I meet you at the sutler's store when I'm off duty. That's it over there." He pointed to a long log building. "It used to be a storehouse for the fur company. We'll have a drink and I'll fill you in on our problems here."

The white men had brought many problems with them by selling alcoholic drinks to the Indian tribes. Traders had cheated the Indians by partly filling the cup with liquor or by holding a finger with two fingers in it or using a small cup with its bottom filled with tallow or by diluting the mixture with more water. Drunken warriors had tried to kill the traders and steal their horses and mules. The whole Indian camp, men, women, and children had run from lodge to lodge drinking and ejecting the content of their mouths into another, whooping, singing, out of control. When the Indians became too obnoxious at the trader's store, the store-keeper built fires of buffalo chips and the smoke drove the Indians out coughing and choking. They soon returned seeking blankets, tobacco, calico, knives, guns, powder balls, combs, mirrors, rings, glass beads, and vermillion paints.

When Pete first arrived there was a tent city in which the soldiers lived but finally adobe and log buildings replaced it. Permanent buildings took almost a year to build.

Peter wrote to Caroline saying that she could come in the summer of 1850. By then the infantry company would move into a new large stable and the mounted companies were to be housed in a new barracks built for one company. By December the first officer's quarters known as "Old Bedlam" would be almost completed. He would have separate quarters by the time she came, small but furnished and having a fireplace to keep them warm. "You must know," he wrote, "that winters out here are so cold that the men on patrol duty wear buffalo robes and blankets and you would not know they were soldiers at all. But inside, dear, our adobe quarters keep us cozy and warm and you, my love, will keep me warmest of all. There are only a few women here, the seamstresses and launderesses and several officer's wives. They are mostly foreign-born. The sutler's wife is one other. I know you will like Iris Delaney. She is the sergeant's wife. She has much the same background as you and has urged me to get you to come. We are constantly in demand by the wagon trains to help with questions raised about the Indians or routes west. The blacksmith Karl Swenson is often busy repairing the many broken wagons that come into the fort. The Mormons are still coming in large numbers anxious to get to their Zion in Utah Territory. I admire their courage but cannot understand their religion. They are fairly well equipped and clean and well-mannered."

Letters between Peter and Caroline were long getting to their destination and she often wrote two or three before she heard from him. He was glad she could stay with her parents and help her father and brothers in the store but he missed her badly.

James Bordeau had been the main trader at the fort and had a Brule wife. He was close to the Sioux and understood their problems. He had left the fort when the army took over and now had another American Fur post up the Platte. Peter had met him one day when Bordeau had ridden into the fort to see the sutler's agent. He was a short, stock Frenchman with a round face and dark moustache. He usually wore a baggy, unpressed suit and vest. He was not known for his valor in his dealings at the fort.

Caleb, the old mountain man who had made the fort his home, had little praise for Bordeau. He told Peter how Bordeau had found that his helper Pierre had been serving good steaks to his friends and himself. Bordeau hid in his store and startled the old man with a ghostly voice warning him not to take any more good beef. Pierre had fainted and knocked himself out and Bordeau had to revive him. When the Indians brought their furs to the fort they fired their guns in a friendly salute outside which was returned by a volley behind the enclosure.

Near the fort was Squaw Town where the Indian squaws lived with their children and wandering braves. There the soldiers and officers from the fort went to see the squaws that their fathers and braves had offered to them. Up stream from the fort were the Oglala Sioux under Chief Smoke who lived from trading with the fort and emigrants and catering to the soldiers at the fort. Some of the Indian girls like Bright Star worked as servants in the officers' quarters, and some were just hangers-on at the fort.

Peter soon learned that the Indian women had ways of getting food and trinkets. They organized dances in front of the

41

officers' quarters where they were lounging on the porch or balcony of their bachelor lodgings. They were accompanied on the drums by old Indian men. They were generally old squaws dressed in buffalo robes who danced around shaking rattles and tree branches. They were rewarded with gifts of flour, meat and rice from the commissary.

The young Indian women were quite attractive in their beaded costumes and some of the men became quite attached to them and wanted to marry them. Squaw Town was a sordid place where the braves felt themselves above menial work and the women employed on the base could not buy the high-priced goods at the army store. They had to scrounge for food from the garbage at the fort.

The emigrant trains brought many pretty eastern girls to the fort and the soldiers enjoyed their chance to associate with them and be in a detachment to accompany them a few miles west. But their ardor was not rewarded by the army commander who confined them to their quarters as punishment if they strayed too far.

The privates made $13 a month most of which was spent at the sutler's store. A poker game was always in progress in the back room. The mountain men used the fort as headquarters and teamsters on wagon trains and civilian employees of the quartermaster were frequent participants in the game.

Peter soon heard that drinking was in excess and was a big problem to the officers and the post commander. To reduce drinking in the sutler's store the names of men were kept on a board with pegs to keep track of the number of drinks each man had. There were frequent quarrels and noisy carousals and military discipline was strict and enforced to take care of the problem. For small offenses the soldiers were assigned extra guard duty or loss of rank. More serious offenses resulted in a soldier being tied to one of the cannons on the parade ground or to be dunked in the Laramie River which was especially dreaded in the cold of winter.

Peter once had to chastise a new private for being drunk and not reporting for drill. Every day the soldiers were drilled on the parade ground and the new recruit had stayed too long in the sutler's store gambling and drinking. When he arrived at the drill, Ned was instructing the men in the use of their muskets in combat. The private was staggering and threatening the nearest soldier and Peter had the provost marshal remove him from the ranks.

"Private Stover," Peter told him, "if you want to attack anyone attack the enemy. You would be of no use to the army in your condition."

Private Stover, his speech slurred by drink babbled, "Damn this out of the way place here. There are no white women only plains, sand and mountains. Hell of a place, dirty savages, danger, hard work, cold and loneliness. Enough to drive a man to drink."

Peter said sternly, "Provost Marshal take him to the guardhouse for a few days. Private, we are all here under army orders and have the same problems. I hope you will learn to live with them. Maybe a few days with bread and water will make you appreciate the food the army sends to us."

If a soldier was under court martial he had to work at hard labor under guard with a ball and chain. Later he might be dismissed from the army and have his insignia ripped from his uniform in front of the entire post and then sent away while the band played, "The rogues March."

The post commander encouraged church attendance which the post chaplain conducted every Sunday. The post library had several hundred books and Peter was an avid reader. The magazines were a month old by the time they arrived but Peter looked forward to seeing how the eastern press was assessing the situation in the west and along the Oregon Trail.

There was a baseball team and Peter played first base on the officer's team. The non-coms and privates tried hard to beat their superiors and often ended up with the trophy given to the winners. Ned Delaney led the team and he and Peter exchanged friendly words about the rivalry between them. Ned had joined the army in the east after coming from Ireland and had been transferred to Fort Leavenworth and then sent out to Fort Laramie before the army had taken over the post. He had risen through his own efforts to be a sergeant. He was a friendly, gregarious young man of twenty-five years but his early rigid training had made him a strict disciplinarian and kept the men under his leadership as much as possible. Peter had taken an instant liking to him and admired his strength and courage. They both agreed on the problems of the post and tried to find ways of preventing trouble which the varied people who came to the fort presented.

Ned's wife Iris had joined him at the fort in the spring of 1850. She was a friendly girl with the same red hair as Ned, a face sprinkled with freckles which the hot Wyoming sun of summer had made even more noticeable. They fit each other like Ned said, "as smooth as a kid glove." Peter enjoyed their company and hoped that when Caroline came they could be good friends.

Night guard duty was the most dreaded assignment for the soldiers. For two hours they kept watch and the shout of "All's well" rang out regularly. Failure to give the call or going to sleep on watch brought a severe penalty for the offender. With the ever-possible Indian attack the Fort had to be on constant alert. The bitter cold winters made this the worst of all. The winds that swept off the Laramie plains made the assignment difficult. The soldiers wore buffalo robes, Indian blankets or any heavy covering to protect them from frostbite. The corporal hauled out a new sentry from his warm bunk every two hours. Heavy gloves on their hands and a fur cap were needed to protect the guard against the bitter cold wind which sometimes fell to 25 degrees below zero.

There was such a feeling of boredom and loneliness in this out-of-the-way post and especially for those who had lived more exciting lives in the east that it was hard to overcome. Peter was well aware of the soldier's feelings for at times he shared their frustration. Many men gave up and deserted their duty and disciplinary problems were common and kept the provost marshal busy.

Many Indian agents became rich defrauding the Indians of their annuities and lands. They plied them with whiskey diluted with water and they became even more susceptible to the white men's greed. They were starved, infected with disease and mistreated by the white men. Many Indian agents took the job only to get rich at their charge's expense. Others tried to understand some of the Indian's problems and hoped to promote peace between the Indians and the whites.

Some of the officers and men became friendly with nearby Indians and visited their lodges to try their dog feasts. Some said the meat was tasty. At least it was a change from the salt pork, beans, jerked beef, and fried vegetables the army served at their mess. The vegetables were sent in hard dried bricks to be freshened by boiling in water.

Depending on the situation at the time the fort went on its usual business and details of men were sent out to obtain wood for the fireplaces and stoves for winter and to harvest the wild hay up the river as food for the many animals at the fort. Sometimes when the Indian braves were on the warpath the soldiers cutting hay had to protect themselves with breastworks of willow branches and any protection such as an enclosure of wagon boxes were used on the wood detail when a small band of Indians attacked. The Indians would give a war whoop and then ride down on the soldiers who sometimes taken by surprise would get their rifles and take a shot at the Indians just as they were disappearing over the hills. It made work on the farm and hay field and wood detail very hazardous and the men were not too happy to be sent on these details when the Indians were on a rampage.

Peter and all the soldiers knew they were out here in the middle of Sioux, Blackfoot, and Cheyenne country without much protection from thousands of Indians who were angry at their enemies. It took brave men to occupy such a position. As usual the army was lax in keeping them supplied with good fighting equipment. The percussion cap gun primer had been in common use since the 1820's but Fort Laramie was still only equipped with flint-lock muskets and accompanying ammunition. The changes in battle weapons were slow in coming to the western outposts.

Now the fort on the Laramie raised its stars and stripes every day and the soldiers practiced their drills on the parade ground. The Indians had been told that the soldiers were to protect them against the intrusions of the whites. They complained to the fort's commander and Peter and all the officers particularly about the loss of buffalo which was their main source of food and livelihood.

In the spring of 1849 Indian Agent Thomas Fitzpatrick had left Fort Laramie with a plan for a great council and an annuity system to pay the Indians for their lands. This plan would make the Indians dependent on the government but would help to quell their resentment and preserve the peace. He met Colonel David D. Mitchell, Superintendent of all western Indian country and told him of his plan. Mitchell who was a long time Indian agent with service in the west and the Mexican War urged Fitzpatrick to go to Washington. There he secured the approval of both the new Secretary of the Interior and the Indian commissioner to call a council of Indian tribes in the summer of 1850.

Upon his return he began visiting the various tribes and telling them about the "Big Talk." Mitchell told all his agents and subagents as well as the fur traders in the territory to tell the Indians that "The Great Father would be fair to them and pay for the destruction of their game, timber, and grass caused by the emigration west." He hoped by these messages to keep the Indians under control.

Peter learned of Fitzpatrick's plan and like most of the other officers approved of it. He admired the Indian agent, an Irishman and a man of excellent experience with General Fremont's and Kearney's expeditions, a good woodsman and mountain man and knowledgeable about the Indian culture and a wilderness guide. He wrote to Caroline of his hope for Fitzpatrick's plan but was disappointed when in 1850 a bill authorizing such a conference was defeated in the House of Representatives. Fitzpatrick was disgusted with the government. He wrote an impassioned plea to Mitchell telling him what the immense migration had done to Indian country and saying that 20,000 well-armed Indians would wreck havoc on future westward travelers.

For this Fitzpatrick was dismissed. The Missouri delegation upheld him and he was reinstated later. Peter was too angry at the intrangience of the government. He had seen the great destruction caused by the flood of emigrants coming west in 1849. His Indian friends, Long Feather and Gray Cloud, had told him of their anger at the debris left along the trail by the thousands of travellers. Long Feather was a tall, well-built Sioux with unusually good features and well-mannered, but he complained about the scarcity of buffalo near the fort.

"Now," he said. "We have to travel far to get meat and robes for our lodges. White men kill for tongues. My children cry for food and there are no buffalo here."

But fear of the Great Father's soldiers and their cannon had spread throughout the tribes and although the red men still harassed the emigrant trains they did not directly attack the fort. An uncomfortable feeling of isolated danger made the soldiers at the fort restless. Peter kept busy with his duties inspecting various army equipment and directing the building of the new barracks and quarters."

Chapter 4A

Caroline Travels West

Caroline had to take the Lake Erie Railroad to Buffalo from New York. Her brothers, Harry and Jed and her father and mother took her to the station and waited until she could board the train. Mrs. Rushton still had misgivings about Caroline's trip to Laramie. She had read so many things about the dangers in the west that she was reluctant to see her leave. She hugged her tightly and kissed her goodbye. "Let us know when you get there safely," she said, "and be very careful."

"I will," said Caroline, "and don't worry there are many women going west now and I am strong and healthy. I can't wait until I see Peter."

"Goodbye dear," said her father. "We will miss you very much and will pray that you get there safely."

Her brothers went to see that her bags were taken aboard and she told them, "Take good care of ma and pa. I will miss you all dreadfully, Helen and Margaret, Susan and Carol, and young Jed and Harry. I love you all."

They bade their goodbyes and Caroline got on the train and waved to them from the car windows. She was on her way to Peter.

She was thrilled by the sight of Lake Erie as they skirted its southern shore. A heavy-set matron, modestly dressed with a big carpet bag came and sat next to her. A summer rain obscured the lake.

"Hello," the lady said. "I am going west to California to join my husband who was bitten by the gold bug last year and joined an expedition to California. He hasn't had too much luck there but some of the men have really struck it rich. Mr. Sutter is building a fort and Horace hopes to get work there. He is a good carpenter and builder. I hated to leave our home but I had to sell it. We have two grown children but they moved to Ohio so I was all alone."

Caroline was sympathetic. "I'm going to join my husband too," she said. "He is a second lieutenant in the army at Fort Laramie."

"Oh dear," said the motherly gray-haired woman. "You are so pretty to be traveling alone. I have heard dreadful stories about those western forts, the Indians and the danger there. I hope everything goes well for you. The conditions in the California gold fields are really primitive to but I am a tough old girl, used to dealing with unpleasant conditions. Horace is sure I can face it. My health is very good for my age."

"You look very well," Caroline said. "My mother is near your age and she has been worried about my decision to join my husband. I am sure I can meet the trials that come. I love Peter so much and he wants me to be with him. There are only a few wives there but more come to visit and there are always a lot of emigrant women going west to meet when they pass the fort."

"When they close the train windows in the rain," the older lady said, "it gets very humid and the ventilators are doing no good. I will be glad when the rain stops and we can get some air. I am happy to get away from the hot dusty streets in New York though."

Caroline said, "We have to change to the Michigan Southern Railroad which takes us to Buffalo."

The plump lady replied, "From Buffalo we take the Lake Shore train to Cleveland. Sure is a lot of waiting at depots and changing trains. Then we'll get to Toledo and change cars for Chicago. I really hate having to make so many changes and seeing that my bags go with me. We will see a lot of scenery though. My sister says the Illinois country is just getting settled and cultivated. The new farms are just beginning to produce crops."

"We stay overnight at Quincy and then take the steamboat to Hannibal, Missouri," Caroline said.

"That will be a change," the lady said. "I'm going to close my eyes and rest until we reach the next stop."

They arrived at all the train stops and had no trouble changing trains. As they neared Hannibal they saw islets covered with trees and blue bluffs that reached for miles on either side. As they came to Hannibal the boat grounded and they were sent ashore. The train backed down to within forty feet of the ship and the passengers got aboard in half an hour. There they saw the Missouri River whose water was like thick milk porridge with deep rapids and drifting logs and trees.

Caroline was glad to have her new friend to talk to as they traveled through a woody ravine westward to St. Joseph which was over two hundred miles distance and took twelve hours to reach. The train puffed its way over the prairies that were five to twenty miles long. Rolling ridges covered with white oak could be seen along the way. The town of St. Joseph was located on the bend of the river, partly on an interval and partly on the southward slope of the bluffs which rose abruptly from the river bank. Here many wagon trains were being outfitted for Fort Hall, Fort Laramie, Green River, and Santa Fe.

Caroline and her friend were surprised at the number of emigrants there. Twelve ox teams headed for the Salt Lake Valley were camped out of town. Tents of gold seekers dotted the landscape. The white canvas of moving trains could be seen in the west like hundreds of ships on the sea. The older lady said, "Horace has made arrangements for me to go with one of the trains to California so I must hurry and find Captain Clark who is the captain of the train I will join. I will miss you dear but since you are taking a stage coach I must leave you. Good luck on your trip from here. It has been nice meeting you and I hope you have a safe journey to Fort Laramie."

"Thank you," Caroline replied. "I will never forget you. May I call you Amanda? I hope the gold fields will furnish Horace with his share of the gold strike and that he will realize his dream."

"Goodbye dear," Amanda said and kissed Caroline on the cheek. "You remind me so much of my daughter Emily. I don't know when I will see her again."

Caroline replied, "Goodbye, it has been nice to have you with me. I will miss you. I have to spend a night at the hotel here and tomorrow a coach will leave for Fort Leavenworth. Peter has some friends there. He was stationed there for six months before being ordered west."

Caroline had a porter carry her bags to the hotel and she entered the small rooming house to get a room for the night. A yawning clerk gave her a key to a room on the second floor.

He said, "Mrs. Meade, will you be staying long? We have had so many emigrants coming and going that I have had very little sleep the last few weeks."

Caroline surveyed the unpreposing array of soiled victorian furniture and seeming lack of good taste and said firmly, "No, I am leaving on the coach for Fort Leavenworth in the morning."

"Well," said the dark haired young man, "we have so many people in town preparing to go west that we like to have reservations in advance. All the hotels in town are full. I'll have a porter take your bags upstairs."

Caroline climbed the dismal-looking stairs and the porter opened a door into a room filled with nondescript furniture. The walls had recently been whitewashed and the bed had clean linen so that it looked fairly habitable. She was glad to be in a room at last. The trip on the trains had been uncomfortable and dirty with the cinders, smoke, and rain.

She lay down on the bed and thought of Peter and how she wished he were here now. She would shower him with kisses, tousel his dark hair and then fall into his arms. She could remember the first night they had spent together after they were married and how tender and considerate he had been. She fell asleep quickly and was so exhausted she was only awakened by the movement of the occupants in the adjoining room who had risen early to catch a wagon train for the west.

She arose, dressed in her brown calico dress and leather boots and went downstairs to a hearty breakfast of ham, scrambled eggs and hot biscuits and then caught the stage across from the hotel.

The stage drive Ira Hodges was a bearded gray-haired man

of middle age. He spat tobacco out of a brown stained mouth over a straggly beard and called to all who wished to take the coach to get in for it was leaving soon.

"Hello," he addressed Caroline, "I'll put your bags on top of the coach. Are you going west from Fort Leavenworth? I am going all the way to Fort Laramie. I am driving the first coach west and am taking dispatches and gold for the army."

Despite his rough appearance he seemed like a friendly man, his bright blue eyes were sharp and honest and seemed to twinkle at her. They reminded her of her father's eyes.

"Yes," Caroline replied. "I'm going on to Fort Laramie. My husband is stationed there. I am going to join him."

"I must warn you," Ira said, "that the road isn't too good to Fort Leavenworth. It rained several days ago and the road west of the fort to Salt Creek is very miry. For a government post in the vicinity the roads aren't very good. We have to watch out for Indians too. Several bands of Kiowa braves are on the warpath and the Pawnee, Sioux and Arapaho too. There are many emigrant wagons on the trail though and we won't be alone. I'm an old experienced teamster and know all the hazards ahead of us. I've made the run many times by wagon, first time with a coach but I know the dad-burned mules. The California Trail keeps along the highest divides on prairie swells to avoid as many bottoms of streams and ravines as possible. Can't stand all the folderol of these settled towns. Like the open spaces best."

"Good," said Caroline. "I will feel safe with you."

There were two other occupants of the coach, a young recruit going to Fort Leavenworth and a pretty blonde girl with curly hair who was also going to the fort. She was obviously trying to be friendly with the young man.

"Hello," she said to Caroline and then started a conversation with the soldier.

"Are you going to Fort Leavenworth?" she asked him. "That's where I'm going."

"Yes," said the young man. "I have been assigned there. I just graduated from West Point. It is my first post."

"Oh, I've been there before," the girl said. "It is a much nicer place than the forts farther west. My name is Helen Porter."

"Have you been to Fort Laramie?" Caroline asked.

"I have heard many stories from soldiers who have come back from there," said Helen. "It is such a boring, lonely post with many Indians and their problems."

"Oh dear," said Caroline. "I'm going there. I hope it isn't too bad. I want to be with my husband Peter."

"Well you just have to get used to it," Helen said. "I've been around and I have learned to get along in these army posts."

She directed her attention again to the young soldier and

Caroline closed her eyes and dozed as the coach rattled along. They crossed from Lawrence, Kansas over the Kaw River. Ira was cracking his whip and yelling at the mules to get them in line, and on board the ferry. The coach was new and was brightly painted with an intricate design on the side. They descended the Missouri bluffs to the muddy river which the Sioux called the Katapan Mine Shoska. The three passengers had to get out of the coach in difficult places to lighten the load but Caroline enjoyed the change for then she could get back the circulation in her cramped legs. Down the steep-banked ford they had to let themselves descend by clinging to a tree, crossing a deep swirling pool in the water on a twisted log. Caroline hired an Indian who was nearby to bring a pony to carry her across and the baggage in the coach was taken over in a skiff.

They had seen many wagon trains on the road and some were having difficulty in crossing streams and needing the help of other teamsters and oxen to cross. Many decided to camp along the trail for the night an go on the next day. The sight of dozens of these canvas topped wagons crossing the prairies with their undulating landscapes reminded Caroline of the sailing boats in the harbor at home. It was a constant reminder of how many people were seeking riches or a new life in the west. The coach stopped occasionally to allow the passengers to rest and Caroline chatted with the women on the trail. The men were feeding their cattle while the women were cooking, sitting beside wagons or washing clothes. She noticed that the oxen were lean and wild-looking, many of them coming from Texas and some still had not learned to pull the big wagons without trouble. There was a loud yelling and swearing as the drivers tried to keep them in line. Many teamsters were unfamiliar with the animals and the problems of the trail. This group was from Ohio and their mired wagon stopped other vehicles from crossing the creek.

From Lawrence which was 35 miles from Fort Leavenworth the trip took eight hours. Fort Leavenworth was the largest place in Kansas and Caroline was amazed at the extensive barracks, capacious storehouses, the several companies of soldiers, the fine houses for the officers, and the huge settler's farm of 1200 acres that the soldiers cultivated. Later Russel, Majors, and Waddel would have acres of wagons, pyramids of axletrees, herds of oxen and many drivers and employees here.

The huge contractor's wagons going to Fort Leavenworth had extra axle trees lashed under the body for with the heavy loads as much as fifty hundred pounds for the fifteen hundred pound wagon made it difficult travelling over the muddy terrain. The early spring rains were making traveling difficult and many wagons were stalled and had to be pulled out by more oxen.

A steamboat came down the Kaw from Fort Riley another

army base. Caroline said goodbye to Helen and Private Harris at Fort Leavenworth. Helen was staying with a friend Lizzie who found the life here was better than she had known before in New York.

Ira knew the owner at the hotel who took Caroline's bags and helped her get a room. The lunch at the hotel consisted of bacon and greens, bread, apple sauce, and pie.

Ira was holding over for a day to get new passengers going west and to take some money and dispatches from the fort to Fort Laramie. Some disillusioned gold-seekers were here, returning east after a disappointing try at finding the rich metal in California.

Caroline asked a soldier where she could find Colonel Ashworth, who had been Peter's friend. He directed her to the officer's quarters. She walked thru the drill ground and was ogled by several soldiers for she was an attractive girl and many of them would have approached her but her modest dress and poise made her an unlikely object of their attention. A sergeant directed her to the officer's quarters of Colonel Ashworth where she was met at the door by an attractive middle-aged lady, the colonel's wife.

"Is Colonel Ashworth here?" she asked. "I am Lieutenant Meade's wife and he asked me to visit Colonel Ashworth when I came through Fort Leavenworth. They were friends when Peter was here."

"Come in," Mrs. Ashworth invited. "Glen will be back soon. They were having an officer's meeting to decide if they should send more men and arms to Fort Laramie and the other western forts."

Caroline entered the room which was modestly but tastefully furnished and decorated with little touches of feminine handwork.

"The Indians are still causing trouble because of the rush of emigrants west in '49 and their ravage of the Indian's lands and buffalo, grass, and timber," the colonel's lady said. "The officers here are always worried about conditions farther west."

"I haven't heard from Peter while I have been traveling," Caroline said, "but he has written about the problems at Fort Laramie and I know that it is hard for the soldiers there."

"While we are waiting would you like a cup of tea and a piece of my dried apple pie?" Mrs. Ashworth asked. "You are really a brave girl to go to Fort Laramie for only a few wives have followed their husbands there. I agree with you though. It is the right thing to do. Glen was in several campaigns when I was in the east and when he was assigned to Fort Leavenworth I couldn't wait to take the first train west."

She made black tea in a big brown stone pot and poured a cup for Caroline and herself.

"The pie isn't my best," she said, "but Glen enjoys it after the years he spent at the army mess. Call me Hazel, dear."

"It is very good," Caroline replied. "The tea is so refreshing. I was tired after jolting over the prairie in the coach and it really hits the spot."

"Here comes Glen now," Hazel said as the colonel came up the steps.

"Dear," she said to him as he entered, "this lovely girl is Caroline Meade, the wife of Lieutenant Peter Meade. She is going out to be with her husband at Fort Laramie."

"Oh," said the colonel who was a handsome middle-aged man with dark hair and aristocratic bearing. "Peter's wife. We have only praise for Peter's stay here at Fort Leavenworth. He was a splendid officer, and well respected by the other officers and the men under him. He will be delighted to see you. My own wife has been so much comfort to me." He hugged his wife around her waist. "That is the height of conjugal devotion to follow your husband to these posts, especially at the one at Fort Laramie."

"I miss him so much and I am sure despite the many problems that I can adjust to the situation there," Caroline replied.

"Will you stay and have supper with us?" they both asked. "Mrs. Brown at the hotel is a good cook but we would be delighted to have you with us. We have many questions about the people in the east and what is going on there. How they feel about the army and its posts and the Indians, the gold rush to California and the opening of Oregon territory," the Colonel said.

Caroline replied, "Thank you. I'd be happy to answer any questions that I can. We saw hundreds of emigrants traveling west. No wonder the Indians are worried. A lot of them were Mormons going to Utah. They seemed to be well-organized and the people were hard-working and pleasant. Ira stopped by one camp for a rest and I was surprised after hearing so much prejudice against them in the east to find they are very much like us. It is a very hard journey west and they still found time to sing and dance in the evenings. Several times we heard clarinets and violins playing their music just before dark and saw their campfires and circles of wagons."

"They are a peculiar people in some ways," the colonel said, "but they are industrious and a capable group. We hear from the west that it is remarkable what they have accomplished in three years in the desert valley of the Great Salt Lake. Jim Bridger was there. He wants to help guide some of our army expeditions west. He is a very experienced mountain man having spent many years crossing the Rockies and living with the Indians and he has married a flathead and several Shoshone wives."

"Peter has written me about meeting Jim Bridger at Fort Laramie. He has many stories to tell about the mountains west of there," Caroline said.

Caroline enjoyed the meal that Hazel had prepared and talked with them both about their mutual interests. The colonel accompanied here back to the hotel saying, "We can't have such a pretty girl out alone with all these soldiers around. They get lonely to have a conversation with anyone from the east. Sometimes they drink too much and then they overstep their bounds."

Caroline bid him goodbye saying, "I will tell Peter how nice you and your wife were to me."

"Give him my regards," the colonel said. "I hope the army there can keep the lid on the Indian-emigrant problems. We are caught between following orders from the Department of the Army and keeping peace between two opposing forces. Some people in Washington haven't the slightest idea of what it is like out here."

Early the next morning Ira knocked on her door and called, "Mrs. Meade, Caroline, breakfast is ready. The stage will leave at 7 for Fort Kearney." He was gone down the hall his stiff leather boots clacking on the bare wooden floor to see that the mules were hitched onto the stage at the stable.

The stage pulled up in front of the hotel exactly at seven and Caroline boarded it. Several new passengers were waiting to get in the coach. Henry Masters was a salesman and was a well-dressed middle-aged man with a bald head and sharp dark brown eyes. Elise Caruthers an older lady with a purple velvet bonnet and fashionable clothes took her seat next to Caroline. Three young soldiers who had been ordered west to Fort Hall came up next and threw their bags up to Dave Mathews, a tall, well-built young man who was riding up with Ira as a guard because they were now carrying a box of gold coins to pay the soldiers in the western forts and some dispatches for the commanders there. All of the men were equipped with rifles.

Chapter 4B

Caroline Arrives at the Fort

Peter was waiting expectantly at the gate of the fort as Caleb, the old mountain man who had become his friend called out to him as he spat a chew of tobacco into the sandy ground. "Peter, thar comes the stage now, the missus will soon be here. They are making good time today."

Peter waited as the coach rattled to a stop kicking up a cloud of blinding dust in its approach. Ira jumped down and tied the reins and went to open the door to let Caroline and the other passengers get out. Henry helped Elise to get down for the long ride had cramped her legs.

Caroline, tired and dusty, emerged to be swept up in Peter's arms. She had never looked so desirable to him. Her dark brown eyes sparkled despite the pressure of the long tedious journey.

"Oh Peter darling, we are together again. I missed you so." she whispered.

"Me too," he said. "Come on to Old Bedlam and see my quarters and you can freshen up. You must be tired after the long trip. But first meet Caleb, my friend, who has taught me many things about the west and the Indians and our problems here."

She extended her hand politely to Caleb whose beard was tobacco stained and who grabbed her hand with his workworn grimy hand.

"Howdy Mam." he greeted her. "Peter here is tops with me. He's taught me about soldiering and I've taught him a few things about the west and Indians and life out here. He was a real green horn at first but he's learning fast."

"Thanks," said Caroline. Peter has written me about your kindness to him."

Caleb was thinking, "She's a real pretty little thing and friendly too."

"Pete sure knows how to pickem." He had chosen to accept the offer of friendship from an Indian chief and had married Lonely Dove a Blackfoot girl who had died in childbirth and was now lodged with a new wife, a Brule, Sioux named Waiting Star. Indian ceremonies had united them in marriage. Waiting Star was a good wife, keeping the tepee neat and clean, drying the buffalo meat he brought back from the hunt and making their clothes from the hides of antelope and deer. She was doing all the work expected of squaws in the Sioux tribe with good humor and patient care. Next spring a new little papoose would bind them even more closely together. At the fort she could get the care of a doctor if one was needed. He still remembered the pain and suffering of Lonely Dove, the muttering of the squaws who

55

attended her and then the announcement that Lonely Dove and the baby had not lived through the delivery of the child.

Peter took Caroline's bags and she went with him as he ascended the stairs of the quarters. Caleb went back to the store to buy a blanket and then to his lodge outside the fort. There Waiting Star was busy cooking a buffalo stew in a big pot over the fire.

Caroline had met several mountain men coming west and had accepted their less than immaculate appearance and rough ways. But she felt that beneath Caleb's cap of buffalo was a friendly face helpful and good natured. She appreciated the friendship he had given to Peter in adjusting to his life here at Ft. Laramie.

"Come on Caroline, I'll introduce you to the ladies of the fort," Peter said. "They are a special group of women and believe me you will learn to like them."

I'm sure I will," said Caroline.

Several of the soldiers were watching as she and Peter made their way across the parade ground to the officer's quarters.

Just as they were climbing the stairs of Old Bedlam a young pretty Indian girl came down the steps. Peter said, "Caroline this is Morning Star. She is Sergeant Perkins squaw. She comes to visit him at the fort every week. She is a Miniconjou, Sioux. Caroline spoke to Morning Star, "How are you," she asked.

"Me fine, you fine too," asked Morning Star. "Lieutenant Meade is so glad to have you come. Perkins say he very lonely without you."

She slipped past them for her mocassined feet made no noise as she hurried on back to her lodge.

"She is very pretty," Caroline said. "Are many of the men involved with Indian women?"

"Quite a few," Peter answered. "It is lonely out here and the chiefs are anxious to please the white men for it is from them they get the whiskey they crave."

"I hate to see them spoiled by the white men's greed," Caroline said. "Someday they will really rebel."

"The young braves are getting very angry with the emigrants," Peter said. "They hate them for cutting trails across their lands and destroying their grass and buffalo herds. They are dependent on the buffalo for food, clothing and shelter and now they are being slaughtered for their tongues or hides."

"Peter, you used to talk of punishing the Indians for harassing the emigrants and said it was the duty of the army to chastise the savages. You have changed your position since you have been out here."

Peter said, "Caroline, I was only spouting off in ignorance before, now I can see the problems of both sides. The Indians have many grievances. I don't agree with some of the officers who want to punish them for small infractions. The old chiefs like Little Thunder want to have peace but the young bucks are ready for war. We are in a dangerous position here."

"You must tell me all about the tribes and your problems here." Caroline said. "Only then can I understand just what we have to face and only then can I be some help to you."

"Caleb has taught me many things about the west and the Blackfoot and Sioux Indians. He has lived with them and knows how they feel." Peter said. They entered Peter's quarters and Caroline said, "It needs a woman's touch." Everything was in place and it was neat and clean but sparse in furniture and accessories. Peter closed and barred the door to intruders and said, "It has been so hard to go so long without you. I have missed you so I can't wait another minute."

She was disrobing, eagerly responding to their mutual desire.

"Oh Peter," she whispered, "We have been apart too long."

Morning came too soon for Peter and Caroline and the bugler aroused the fort with the day's first call. Peter awoke to find Caroline still sleeping, her long dark brown hair touseled and her naturally beautiful skin made her an object of his desire.

He roused her gently, "Caroline, I have to get up. The men have morning drill in the courtyard and I have to be there."

She opened her big brown eyes, surveyed her new surroundings and sleepily said, "Oh I'm so tired after my journey could I rest just a little longer?"

"Yes, dear," he said, kissing her softly on the lips.

"I will eat breakfast in the mess hall today with the men. I will be back later. Iris, Mrs. Delaney, the Sergeant's wife said she would come in to see you and show you around the fort.

He looked so distinguished as he finished dressing in his uniform she thought and older too. He had matured so much in the months they had been apart, but he was the same dear, considerate lover she had found last night and she admired him for staying true to her.

She slept a short time, then awoke, dressed in a new red calico dress, unpacked her bags, hung up her clothes in a makeshift closet and was ready when Iris knocked on the heavy wooden door of their quarters. She opened the door to see a red-haired, freckled-faced young woman of about twenty-five years standing there.

"Hello, are you Lieutenant Meade's wife," she asked. "I am Iris Delaney, Sergeant Delaney's wife. Welcome to the fort. Life here is unusual to say the least. There are a mixture of soldiers, mountain men, Indians and emigrants coming west who visit or live here. Some think this is a godforsaken post and to come here to our husbands is the height of real devotion. How was your trip west. I hope you will be content to remain so we can be friends." She was holding a chubby little red-haired boy by the hand. "This is Little Ned our son."

She was rushing on as though she had to get everything said. She extended her hand which was red from work and sunburn and freckled like her face. She clasped Caroline's hand tightly and her sincere welcome was reflected in her friendly face.

Caroline knew instantly that she would like her new acquaintance and that she would not be alone now. "I'm so glad to meet you," she responded. "And you too," she said as she patted little Ned on his thick nap of red curls.

"Come over to our quarters and have breakfast," Iris invited. "Then we can go and I will show you the fort. Would you like to see the sutler's store and the rest of the buildings. I can tell you its history. The army only bought it from the fur company in 1849 when Peter came here. The old fort was built by several mountain men and named Fort William after William Sublette.

Caroline followed her to the Sergeant's quarters and Iris poured her a steaming cup of coffee and served her a stack of hotcakes and syrup. Everything tasted so good after the poor food she had sometimes had on the trail. Little Ned sat up on a high chair and Iris cut up his hotcakes which he ate with his fingers.

She kept up her lively chatter telling her about her folks in the east and her husband, Ned. Caroline in turn told of her life in New York and about her family. She learned that Sergeant Delaney had emigrated from Ireland and had met Iris when he was on leave from the army which he had joined as a recruit. They had little Ned two years ago and Iris was pregnant and they expected a baby in the Spring. Iris had come from a large family as had Ned and they both wanted to have a big family. She missed her brothers and sisters but she had accepted the life at the fort and was glad she had come to be with Ned.

"Thank you for the good breakfast," Caroline said. "I have really missed the good home cooking since I left home. Some of the meals at the stops along the trail were good but all were not the best. We crossed the river yesterday and they charged three dollars to let the stage pass over it."

"That's the Laramie River," Iris said. "The North Platte comes in to it nearby."

They went out and Iris said, "Here is the post office where you can mail a letter to your folks. It takes a long time to get east though."

"I know," said Caroline. "Peter's letters were a long time coming."

"Here is the hotel where people stay for short periods when traveling east or west," said Iris. "The Wyoming Hotel is the long log building there."

"And here's the sutlers store where everyone congregates. They have many goods but the prices are high. James Bordeaux used to run the store but he is gone now. He moved to a post about eight miles up the North Platte. There are about one hundred and fifty officers and men here. Some of them get too friendly with me for they are lonely and Ned has to put them in line. Come along dear," she called to Little Ned as he stopped to pet a little black dog by the store.

"We saw many Indians approaching the fort." Caroline said.

"Yes Iris replied. "There are many lodges of the Sioux just outside of the fort and when they come in to sell furs for whiskey they can get very demanding and insolent."

She continued as they approached the sutler's store. "This store is the center of social life in Fort Laramie. When visitors come they find more people here on Sunday than in church. They smoke, drink champagne and whiskey and generally raise hell. When I first came I was never so disappointed in any place in my life. To see a fort situated in a low valley surrounded by high bluffs and such a desolate and lonely place as one could find made me want to go back home. We had been at Fort Leavenworth, not a great post but closer to civilization. Ned came out with Colonel Kearney before Peter came with Major Sanderson. I've been here a year and now I have adjusted to the primitive conditions and with you here I'm sure I'll like it better. I'm so glad you came." She squeezed Caroline's hand as she led her up the steps of the log building.

Several Indians were sitting on stools made of rough wood with buffalo hide seats. Some were along the wall and others were selling furs to the sutler. The soldiers were drilling in squads on the parade ground and Caroline could hear the sergeants calling out loud commands to them.

Iris went up to the counter and the sutler's wife came out to greet her.

"Hello Iris. What can we do for you?" she asked.

"This is Lieutenant Meade's wife, Caroline. She is going to be here with us at the fort."

The sutler's wife, a thin, tall woman of middle-age surveyed Caroline intently and decided she liked the girl's neat pleasant appearance. She came from behind the counter to welcome her.

"Welcome to Fort Laramie, Caroline. Let's dispense with formalities. Out here we soon come to know each other. Has Iris told you about the variety of people here."

"She is taking me around the post and introducing me to everyone we see. It is interesting to meet them. Peter has written me many exciting things about the west and especially here at Fort Laramie." Caroline replied.

"She just arrived by the first coach yesterday," Iris said. "I would like to get more bacon and coffee if I could."

The sutler's wife said to her husband. "This is Lieutenant Meade's wife. She will make a good addition to the women at the fort."

The sutler came forward after dickering with two Indians and met Caroline. He was clad in a dark suit with a beard and dark hair splashed with gray. His black eyes were sharp and penetrating.

"Well the Lieutenant has good taste in women," he said, "to pick such a pretty girl for a missus. Welcome to the fort."

"Thank you," Caroline blushed. "I think I will be here for awhile at least as long as Peter is stationed here."

"Would you slice off a chunk of the bacon that just came in from St. Louis for Iris and give her a can of coffee," his wife asked.

"Please put it on our bill," Iris said. "Caroline, is there anything you need?"

Caroline said, "Peter and I will get things arranged in our quarters and then I'll see what we need and what Peter likes to eat out here. He has changed his diet since being out west and he can help me pick the things we need."

Some of the Indians were still dozing in their seats but two got up and staggered out of the fort to their lodges.

"They do cause a lot of problems when they get liquor in exchange for their furs. The white men have used it to cheat many of them," Iris said.

"Later some of them may pay for their dishonesty," Caroline replied, but both sides are to blame for the situation."

They went outside to see some emigrants arguing over what they must leave behind here at the fort for the trip over the mountains. Their wagons were overloaded and Jim Bridger, the mountain explorer, had advised them to adjust their load before starting over the divide. He told them, "See that peak. That was just a hole in the ground when I first came here."

"Is that the famous Jim Bridger we hear about in the east?" Caroline asked.

"Yes, said Iris. He has built a fort down on the Green River. He has had an Indian wife from the Flathead tribe named Cora and two Shoshone and is friendly with the Indians especially the Utes."

He was dressed in buckskin clothes and hat and was not a tall man but well built. Caroline decided that he was a typical mountain man, hardened by years of roaming the mountains living with the Indians and adapting to their ways. Living such a precarious life must be only for the most adventuresome men, she decided.

"They will do well to take his advice," Iris said. "He knows this western country as well as any."

After angrily agreeing to leave one of her prized possessions, a small piano, the emigrant lady went inside with her husband, a tall, thin, poorly clothed man to see if the sutler would buy it from them.

Now that Caroline had met the famous mountain man Jim Bridger she was anxious to know more about this experienced western explorer and scout who had traveled widely in the mountain. Peter had told her that Bridger had built a fort in the Black's Fork region of Wyoming Territory in the summer of 1842. First he had built buildings overlooking Black's Fork on the bluff but after less than a year he had abandoned this place and moved in August 1843 to the river bottoms. Here was an ideal place for an emigrant trading post between the mouth of the Big Sandy and the Black's Fork River in southwest Wyoming. Here grass was plentiful and fresh water, mountain trout and cottonwood timber were available. The fort had been built of poles, dogwood branches and mud. The Shoshone Indians had built about twenty-five lodges there too with many trappers with Indian wives. Here could be brought robes, dressed deer, elk and antelope skins, coats, pants, moccasins and traders would barter them for flour, pork, powder, lead, blankets, butcherknives, spirits, hats, ready made clothes, coffee, sugar etc. At Fort Bridger they kept a herd of cattle and twenty or thirty goats.

Caroline said, "It must have been a good place for the emigrants, especially the Mormons to stop before going on down into the Great Salt Lake Valley.

Peter replied, "It was a favorable place for Bridger and his partner Louis Vasquez, a Mexican citizen to build a fort but various problems came to plague them and Jim liked to travel back east and scout for the army and the different expeditions who came into the hills."

Caroline said, "He seems like a very resourceful man and must be really brave to spend so much time among the Indian tribes and exploring the mountains."

Peter had told her, "He will long be remembered for his work in opening up the west. It takes a really hardy man to survive the difficulties he has been through. He has two adjoining log houses with dirt roofs and small picket fence of logs about eight feet high. Caleb says he has been to visit him but Jim was often away on trips. His first wife died four years ago. She was the daughter of the Flathead chief, Insula and then he married his second wife a Snake squaw in 1849 just a year ago. They had a severely cold winter two years in 1848-49 which was hard on their cattle and people. The drifts of snow were fifty feet deep."

"It must have been a very bitter winter," Caroline said.

"Yes," Peter said. Caleb was still talking about the harsh winter they had here at Fort Laramie the winter before we came here with Major Sanderson. The next summer, though, the thousands of gold seekers helped the fort's trade and the Mormons were still coming in large numbers. Their missionaries area getting many new members in England and Scandinavia.

61

"How far west from here is it?" Caroline asked.

"About one hundred fifty miles if you take a cut off." Peter said, "But I've never been farther west than about twenty miles into the Black Hills. There are many long stretches of alkali desert and sagebrush through Wyoming and its a rough trip up over South Pass and over the divide and through the Rockies to the Great Salt Lake.

"Mr. Bridger loves to tell stories about his travels," Caroline said. "He keeps the men at the sutler's store interested with his tales when he visits Fort Laramie. Most of the caravans take a weeks rest at Fort Laramie to assess the situation, confer with the other members of the train, do their laundry and adjust their loads for the steep climb over the mountains. Here they could get reliable information about the trip farther west from those who had traveled the route and men who had returned from California. Many wagons that had fallen apart during the journey were left rusting and broken just outside the fort. All the travelers were grateful for a place to spend a quiet night and Sunday listening to the missionaries and the chaplain at the fort and enjoying the feeling of safety with the army here after traveling so long in dangerous country.

The fort became a busy place when the Indians came to bring their furs twice a year to sell at the American Fur post nearby. There James Bordeaux and other traders made deals with the Sioux and obtained their pelts at the best price. They were eager to get whiskey and guns and ammunition and frequently the trader made the best of the deal. Some were permanent hangerson at the fort and the sutler's store was besieged with visitors, the braves and the squaws and their papooses. They came to offer dried pemmican, buffalo tongues, blankets, skins and other Indian wares for sale a week later.

Caroline said to Iris as they were quilting one day, "Look some of the squaws are peering in your window." Little Ned ran to the window and the faces disappeared.

"Don't let it bother you," Iris said. "They come with the braves at trading time. The sutler really has to watch them for they can take anything that isn't nailed down. They even sneak behind the counter and sell their goods twice. They are learning to get even with the traders who have always taken advantage of them, selling them watered down whiskey and then getting their furs for almost nothing. The white men have really been cruel to them bringing them small pox epidemics and cholera and other diseases, killing their buffalo, their main source of livelihood and destroying their grass and trees along the trail. They are very superstitious and curious people and want to see how the white man lives. Some tribes are friendly and some very wary and unhappy at the number of white men coming into their country."

"When we came out," Caroline said, "the roads were

crowded with wagon trains. It seems that everyone wanted to go west. As they went over the hills three and four lines beside each other their canvas tops looked like dozens of ships sailing away on the ocean."

Iris went over to the window and the noses that had been pressed to the glass window were gone.

"Apparently," said Iris, "they are going back to their lodges outside the fort. It must be time to cook their buffalo stew. I hope no more dogs have disappeared. Last time they came one of the sutler's dogs turned up missing. Ned tells me to keep Missy inside when they visit the fort in large numbers." Missy was a little brown and white terrier who was sleeping quietly on a rug near the door. Iris went over and patted her on the back and she jumped up to lick her face and little Ned petted her.

"Oh dear," said Caroline, "that is one thing I can't understand. It seems so cruel to think of eating dog meat."

"Some of the mountain men and Father De Smet, the Jesuit priest who has spent much time traveling among the Indian tribes, says it is quite tasty if you get used to it." Iris answered.

"No time," replied Caroline. "That is one meat I can't eat. Buffalo steaks are quite good when they are from a young animal and well cooked but I couldn't think of eating dog meat."

"After you've been out here associating with all the various people who come to the fort," Iris said, "You begin to realize that our sheltered way of thinking in the east just doesn't prepare you to meet all the problems here. Sometimes the buffalo are getting scarce in the north and the Sioux and the Cheyennes are hungry. The Indian agents are getting worried about the conditions caused by the large number of white men coming into the west. They have greatly increased over last year. The gold rush to California, settlers to Oregon and Mormons to the Great Salt Lake Valley have added to the travelers down the trail.

Peter and Ned have been busy just trying to help and to keep the Indians from revolting. Most of the soldiers here are unhappy at being at such a remote spot and spend a lot of time drinking and gambling. This leads to all kinds of problems for the commander and other officers."

"The Mormons I have met," Caroline said, "are not at all like the eastern papers said. They are a very devout hard-working people. Most of their wagon trains are well organized and well equipped. Some of the general emigrants have a haphazard approach to this move west and have run into a lot of trouble. We saw many instances of poor preparation for such a hard and trying journey."

Iris broke another piece of thread off the spool and pulled it through the thickness of the quilt. Caroline was stitching along the one side nearest to the edge.

"Ned has made me a cradle for the baby and this quilt will

help to keep him warm next winter," Iris said. "It is good of you to help me with it. I am getting so large now that it is hard to sit here very long."

"What does Ned want" Caroline asked. "A girl or a boy."

"Like all fathers he wanted a boy first," Iris said. "He wants a big family. We both come from large families."

"We few wives have to do all we can to understand the problems our husbands face and make it as easy for them as we can." Iris said. "They are daily beset with all kinds of trouble. I hope the council Tom Fitzpatrick is planning for Fort Laramie and his trip to St. Louis to see David Mitchell will result in helping to solve the situation between the Indians and our people. Ned is torn in his sympathy for both sides."

"Peter too," Caroline said as she quilted around the animal block that Iris had embroidered on the quilt. "I can't see how they will ever come together."

"Well the agents hope to get the government to repay the Indians for the loss they have taken but congress is very slow in acting on the measures put before them. A lot of them do not understand all the conditions out here."

"Some of the white men, especially the mountain men, have adapted to the Indian ways. You know that Major Alexander Culbertson at Fort Union has married an Indian princess from a Blood tribe. She is learning to live in a different culture although she still clings to some of her Indian traditions. Her name is Natawista. Major Culbertson was thirty years old when he saw her when she came with the Blood tribe to the fort when she was only fifteen."

"Father Pierre Jean De Smet, the Jesuit priest who has spent more time traveling among the Indian tribes than some mountain men, is going out to visit Fort Union next summer. That is where Major Culbertson lives. His assistant Edwin Denig has an Indian wife too. Her name is Deer Little Woman and she comes from the Assiniboin tribe. Father De Smet wants to encourage Denig to write stories about the Indians, their legends and culture and his experiences at this American Fur Co. post. He has had two Indian wives and has made a thorough study of Indian life. Major Culbertson has imported fine clothes for his wife, fancy foods for her table and candy and toys for his children. They come by boat up the Missouri from St. Louis. Fort Union is located far north on the Missouri. The major is a very learned man and reads newspapers and books on religion and philosophy. He can teach the visitors to the fort about the Indian leaders and can take them to observe Indian life and attend their council. Several famous artists have come to visit the Culbertsons and the Denigs.

"I was so frightened of Indians when I left home, Caroline replied, "and we were attacked by some Kiowas on the way west. That was the most terrifying experience but Ira and Dave and the boys fought them off the rest disappeared into the hills. I am learning to like some of the friendly indians like Bright Star and Caleb's wife and I am learning more about their ways and people and I can understand their problems."

Iris added, "This little quilt will keep our little baby comfy and warm next winter. It has an Indian blanket inside for a filling and the brown and red calico pieces make it quite pretty."

"It's fun to quilt, Caroline said. "Ma taught me when I was only ten. She has made so many pretty quilts. She made Harry and Jed and me one when we were married. I couldn't bring mine west. I have Peter's and my things stored at Ma's and I will be glad when we can make a permanent home and use them. I am quite worried about Pa and I haven't heard from them for so long. I hope the mail will get more reliable out here. I miss all of them so much.

Iris sympathized, "My folks try to keep in touch but it has been months since Ned has heard from his brothers and sisters in Ireland. It was really a great day when I met Ned. He came to a country fair with a cousin and we hit it right off as soon as we met. He was such a big red-headed Irishman with a good sense of humor and a hearty laugh. He just swept me off my feet and I have never regretted a moment even here in Fort Laramie," she laughed. He has been out with the wood detachment the last few days I will be glad when he can meet you."

Caroline said, "It is so wonderful to meet friends like you and Ned. I know how much Peter thinks of Ned and how he depends on his help and advice. It makes all the hard trip and adjustments to frontier life worthwhile and you have taught me so much."

"Tell me more about Major Culbertson and Natawista, Caroline pleaded.

Iris continued, "Many famous people came to visit with the Major and Natawista at Fort Union. John James Audubon the famous artist came in 1843 in search of animals to paint for his collection. At the post wine was served and balls were given and a rare mock buffalo hunt for his pleasure was staged. Natawista rode out dressed in Indian dress with her beautiful black hair floating behind her. She decorated a parfleche with dyed porcupine quills and dove into the Missouri River to bring back six mallard ducks for him to paint. Since he was French and she could speak French and Cree they could converse together. He admired her beauty and domestic skill but could not enjoy seeing her eating raw buffalo brains as her people did. She reverted to her Indian ways when her children were sick and used old Indian remedies to make them well."

"What a fascinating story," Caroline said.

"Yes," Iris continued, "Five years ago Major Culbertson

built a new fort up the Missouri and named it Fort Benton after his friend Senator Thomas Benton of Missouri and three years ago he moved the fort again and built walls of adobe. They are still there. Major Culbertson has a reputation for fair dealing and the Blackfeet, Piegans, Bloods and Gros Ventures bring their beaver skins to him. He is known even in Washington. Ned says he is regarded very highly there for his understanding of Indians and their ways. They have sometimes by spring even bartered their bedding and kitchen cutlery for the skins and the boats going down the Missouri are loaded with furs. Natawista is a big asset to Major Culbertson and travels with him between the fort and the Indian camps. She always goes along to make a home wherever they stop."

Caroline said, "What a remarkable pair of people. I'm sure Peter has heard of the Culbertsons but he has never told me about them."

Iris said, "After they finish their American Fur Business they are going to his estate outside of Peoria, Illinois and build a home. That will be like living in another world for Natawista." It will be like adapting to a different way of life.

"She sounds like a beautiful very resourceful woman," said Caroline. "I only hope it works out for them. It is very hard to bridge two such different cultures."

"At times, Caleb says," Iris replied, "she goes back to her native ways and sometimes longs for her people in Canada."

"Caleb should know for Waiting Star is an example of a good lodge squaw. He took me to see her in their home outside of the fort and she gave me some service berry pudding she had made out of dried berries and flour and buffalo fat. It was very good. Peter has told me not to go now the Indian camps for some of the young warriors are getting restless and want to harass the whites especially the emigrants on the trail. It isn't safe for us to go outside the fort. Waiting Star had everything in order, a big buffalo stew over the fire and Caleb is right at home with her people.

"No, Iris said. "We have to be careful. I used to take a short ride up the trail but there have been several incidents of Indian attacks on lone travelers. Ned and Peter will soon be back. Help me make one roll of the quilt and then we'll leave it to finish tomorrow."

Caroline unpinned the end of the small quilt and together they rolled up the right side. "Another day's work and we will have it done." she said.

Iris replied, "Thanks so much for your help, Caroline.
Several hands make light work. At home we had many more helpers at the church and the big quilts were quickly done.

"Your baby will be comfy under this quilt," Caroline said. "Peter says the winters are really windy and cold here."

"Yes," Iris said. "We even need buffalo robes to keep us warm."

They watched Missy jumping for a ball on the floor and Little Ned running to catch it. Iris showed Caroline a wooden cradle that Ned had made saying, "Ned made this cradle for me. He carved the foot and headboard out of a piece of hard wood he found around the buildings and polished it himself. They are trying to build more barracks which they need badly to house more soldiers."

"Ned does beautiful work," Caroline said. "Peter says the army is checked by the whims of the government. They can't seem to decide what to do about all the problems of developing the west," Caroline answered.

Iris said, "Peter and Ned are caught in a struggle between the Indians and our own people. It is very hard for them. I hope the council next summer will help to solve some of their differences. Ned says some of the Indian agents are getting rich at the expense of their charges and defrauding them of their land and furs. He can understand their anger."

Caroline soon left saying goodbye to Iris to return to their quarters in the big adobe building. She must learn she realized to understand all the problems Peter faced. To adjust to different customs. To be aware of but not frightened by the dangers they might encounter here at Fort Laramie. Iris, with her calm, pleasant disposition, seemed to be able to cope with all kinds of difficulties.

Several days later Caroline took off her brown calico wrapper after getting breakfast for Peter and kissing him as he left to perform his duties on the post. She said, "I'll be at Ned's and Iris's this morning to help her finish the baby's quilt.

"We are meeting with the Commander to assess the problems with the Indians and how best to handle them. Tom is sure he can get the government to pay them for some of their losses. It is hard to get the congress to realize the gravity of the situation. Caleb has been out traveling among the tribes and isn't very hopeful about having peace. Many of the young warriors are restless and pushing for action against the white intruders. Keep close to the quarters inside the fort, dear. It isn't safe to go outside," Peter reminded her.

"I will dear," she said. "It is so good to have a friend like Iris. I hope I get to meet Ned today."

"You'll like that big Irishman as well as I do," Peter said. "You should see him today for his detachment came in last night with several wagonloads of wood to keep the fires burning this winter."

She put on her red calico dress, brushed her long dark brown hair and coiled it neatly around her head. Then she went down the stairs to Iris's quarters and knocked on the wooden door. She

67

heard Iris call, "Almost dressed. Be right there."

Her auburn hair was awry and her ruddy face glistened from a fresh washing as she emerged, cheerful and pleasant. Little Ned was dressed and playing with blocks on the rug near the fireplace.

"Haven't been feeling too well in the mornings," she said. "Takes me a little longer to get going."

"I hope everything is going well," Caroline said. "Peter and I want to have some children as soon as we can. When I came I was frightened of having one out here but since seeing how Ned and you and Little Ned are doing I feel better about it."

"I have to go to the fort's doctor tomorrow and I hope everything is coming along fine," Iris said. "Ned came from a big Irish family and he loves children. Here's the thread and needles and thimble. Caroline would you like to work along the side we rolled yesterday."

Caroline sat down and inserted her thread at the base of the animal block. "It will only be a short time before snow is falling Peter says and then the fort will be isolated by drifts and wind."

"We should get it finished today." Iris said "and then I can put it away with my baby things in the big chest over there. It really gets cold and the blizzards are fierce here. The Indians will be making their winter camps in the most sheltered spot they can find. It must be hard for them to prepare for it but their fires keep their buffalo-hide lodges quite warm. A big band of Miniconjou, Sioux stay outside the fort in their lodges and only occasionally come into the fort to trade or barter for the goods they need. Next spring the emigrants will come and in June and July the rush of travelers will make the fort hum with activity. It makes Ned worry that with so few soldiers here and the Indians should unite what they could do.

"I don't like to think of it," said Caroline. "The army expects so much of its western commanders and its officers some of whom have had little experience out here.

"My family warned me against coming west, the Indians, the buffalo and wild animals, the hard conditions of traveling by coach into the wilderness, across streams and over such rough country where only a few white women have been five years ago. I had to be with Peter and he wanted me to come. I am strong and healthy and I can adjust to conditions here."

Iris replied, "Only a devoted wife would make the trip. A few have come out here and stayed only a few weeks and then joined a group of disgruntled gold seekers going back home and left for good. When I came I decided that I would be here as long as Ned was kept here. I will be glad to return to an eastern post when he goes. He says that most West Point graduates especially those who have good connections avoid coming to these western posts."

Caroline responded, "Peter didn't have anyone who could pull rank for him so he was assigned out here."

Iris got up and went to the window to look out. "Look out there," Iris called. "There comes Caleb on his pinto Indian pony. He must be going to the sutler's store. He is bringing in some skins he has trapped on the river. See he has a Mexican saddle with stirrups as big as coal scuttles and iron spurs that tinkle. Waiting Star, his Sioux wife, must have made his fancy buckskin suit and trimmed it with beads and porcupine quills and put fringe down the sides."

"What's that he's got on his pony?" Caroline asked.

Iris said, "He has a shoulder belt to hold his powder horn and a bullet pouch fastened to various instrument, an awl with a deer horn handle point and his rifle and pistol to protect him from unfriendly Indians. He carries a case made out of cherry wood, a sharp knife and a worm to clean his rifle. That's an short odd-looking bullet mould too with strips of buckskin to protect his hands when running balls and a small bottle made from the scraped point of an antelope horn which contains the scent for baiting the beaver traps. He has learned over the many years to be prepared for emergencies and although he is friendly with the Sioux he never knows when another tribe may attack him. He has been in many hair-raising experiences in his years of traveling in the mountains. Once he was captured and almost scalped by the Blackfeet but was able to escape by night and hide until he could get a horse and get away. He knows just where the few remaining beaver are and how to trap them. He is a "baccy-chewing, cigar-smoking mountain man."

"He has been very helpful to Peter," Caroline said, "and a good friend."

"Ned respects his advice and knowledge about the Indians and his trails west into the Rocky Mountains. He's been west to California and back through the Great Salt Lake Valley."

The laundresses here have a hard job too," Iris continued. "With the harsh lye soap the army uses and trying to keep the uniforms starched properly. Most of them are English, German or Scandinavian and the men make their lives miserable with proposals and invitations. The post band plays at the hotel regularly and they go there to dance with the soldiers. Maren and Greta are quite nice girls and would like to meet a desireable man to marry."

"I've met several of them," Caroline replied, "and even though they don't speak good English yet we find we can talk with one another."

"That's what was hard for me when I first joined Ned here," Iris said. There were so few women on the base. When I heard that you were coming I jumped for joy."

They had finished the quilt and they took it off the frame.

Iris would finish the edge by hand.

Just as Caroline was going to leave they heard a hearty laugh and into the room came Peter and a big red-headed man whom Caroline instantly knew was the Ned that she had heard so much about from Iris. Little Ned jumped up and Ned took him into his arms. Peter introduced them saying, "This is my friend Sergeant Delaney, Caroline, and this little sweetheart is my wife Caroline. I am glad that at last you can meet. Ned has been directing the wood detail and watching out for the renegade Indian bucks who sometimes attack the men and steal their horses. They brought in several wagons of dry fuel last night and the recruits are cutting it up into fireplace logs."

"I am very happy to meet such a good friend of Peter's." Caroline said. Iris has told me so much about you I felt I already knew you."

Ned grabbed her small soft hand in his big rough and calloused one and shook it with a friendly grip. "You are just as Peter described you and I am happy you are here to keep Iris company. Now she is in the family way she has been getting very lonesome for her folks in the east.

"I know how she feels," said Caroline. "Peter, I was just leaving I am ready to go home. Shall we go."

"Pete, boy, you can't miss that chance to be alone. We will see you later," replied Ned.

In September the cold winds blew across the Laramie Plains and the occupants of the fort retreated into sheltered areas. Peter and Ned donned their big buffalo robes to keep them warm as they went around their winter duty. One of the privates brought in a big pile of logs from the wood gathered from the timbered hills and piled it in a small area next to the big door. The fireplace was kept supplied with new logs and only at night did the temperatures drop below zero. Then Peter and Caroline were comfortable under the heavy blankets and buffalo hides that covered them.

Caroline soon learned to make good stew in the big iron pot over the fire and to make biscuits and pies in the covered dutch oven. A huge pot of rich brown coffee was always brewing to one side of the fire. It tasted good in the evenings when Peter came in from the bitter cold outside.

Caroline now had shared all of Peter's daily problems and his knowledge of the Indians and the west. She better understood just how their culture differed from the life of her own people. Bright Star an Indian girl who helped around the fort came and went. Her dark shiny hair hung down in braids held with a colorful beaded band, her buckskin dress was beautifully trimmed with bright beads and porcupine quills. She came now wrapped in an Indian blanket and silently walking in her beaded deerskin moccasins. She performed her duties, sweeping, dusting, straightening furniture and making the bed neatly. She cleaned the fireplace and swept the ashes into a bucket to be removed outside. Caroline observing her neat ways said, "Bright Star do you have an Indian lover? You must know many eligible young Sioux in your camp."

"I wait for one to offer my father some horses for my hand." she said. "Long Lance has said he wishes to marry me. He is a Miniconjou too and is strong and brave and a fine buffalo hunter. We have met in the grove of the quivering leaves to talk together. He rides with some braves who want to attack the fort and kill the yellow hairs and that I cannot see."

Caroline pleaded, "Oh no. I hope the older chiefs can reason with the younger warriors. It would be tragic to have a battle between them. Tell your people that the white soldiers have several cannon that can kill many Sioux. I pray that they will never need to use them."

"There are many, many Sioux," Bright Star said but not too many soldiers but I hope they never war against each other. The Great Spirit does not want them to fight. The soldiers have been good to me and taught me to speak their language. I will beg Long Lance not to ride against the fort."

"Please," Caroline asked. "Tom Fitzpatrick hopes to get the Great Father in Washington to pay for the losses your people have taken. He is going to visit the tribes to get them to meet in council next summer."

"They will come to the council," Bright Star promised. "Little Thunder, our chief, wants to have peace with the white men. He says white men come like hordes of crickets from the east to destroy our land and kill our buffalo. Many have come in the last six moons. Their white wagons have cut many trails through our land."

"They seek gold in California and land in Oregon and the Mormons seek a refuge in the Great Salt Lake Valley," Caroline said.

"My people are sometimes going hungry," Bright Star said. "The buffalo are moving south. Long Lance rides far to get buffalo meat for his mother's lodge. He gets very angry at the white men who are crossing our path."

"We must do all we can to keep peace," Caroline said.

The winter snows and blizzards kept the fort closed in and Peter and Caroline were aware of the isolation. Only when bundled up warmly could she go over to the sutler's store or they could join Ned and Iris at the dance at the hotel. The lively twang of a jew's harp or the squeaky music of the fiddle played by some teamsters wintering at the fort kept the nights from becoming monotonous. The chaplain gave his sermons on Sunday but most of the soldiers preferred the comraderie at the sutler's store.

Iris was being checked by the fort doctor and now was sewing small flannel garments, hoping to have her second born a boy for Ned had four brothers and hoped that it would be a boy. "Sure," he said, lapsing into his Irish dialect. "I'm hoping the Delaney family is blessed with another baby boy."

"Oh you son of the Irishood," Iris said. "How about a dainty little miss so I can sew ruffles on her dresses and put her hair in curls."

"Oh sure and begorra we'll take what we get," Ned said, "and praise the dear Lord if you and the baby come through in fine shape. My girl, you are in fine fettle tonight." He said and kissed her.

One night Peter and Caroline were do si doing to the call of the square dance when Ned and Iris came in to the hotel and Caroline said, "Ned and Iris look so happy tonight. They are such good friends and a dear couple."

"Yes," agreed Peter. "Ned is a fine sergeant. He holds the men in line and they all respect him. He is so much help to me here at the fort. It is no easy job when guard duty is so miserable in the winter but we have to be on the alert for an Indian attack. That big Irishman can bring the recruits into line with one bellow of his powerful lungs. You look especially beautiful tonight dear." Peter added as he squeezed Caroline's hand at the end of the dance. "All the men have been staring at you."

"I am devoted only to you," she told him. "You look so handsome in your uniform without all the winter gear. Let's go over and have a drink of punch and warm ourselves by the big fire in the fireplace. Private Drew has kept the wood bin full of huge logs. See, Iris and Ned are going there too."

Some of the soldiers had been imbibing too freely and were becoming unruly and noisy so the Provost Marshal warned them about their loud talk and improper actions.

One brushed Peter and said, "Lieutenant you must be happy to have such a beautiful lady here on the post. We privates do not have that choice. We are just displaced citizens and targets for Indian arrows."

Peter answered firmly. "All of us have our problems here, Private Drew. The officers all realize the isolation of the fort and how the recruits feel about their duty. We must all try to accept our position and make the most of it."

The soldier moved aside and saluted as Peter and Caroline went on to the punch bowl. Caroline was glad that Peter had handled the encounter with proper control. She knew that his anger was close to the surface now because of all his feelings about the situation here and because the government and the army had not given the needed support to the post.

Caroline soon accepted her new home and learned to adapt

to the change in her life. She eagerly questioned Peter about the Indian tribes nearby and the problems of the army in these outlying posts. He appreciated her concern and the way she had tried to accept their position here at Fort Laramie and make herself a part of his life now.

"Darling," he said one morning as they lay in bed. "You are so sweet and friendly. Everyone who has talked to me admires you and is pleased that you are here."

"Thank you," she said as she kissed him over and over again. That means so much to me. I only feel complete when I am here beside you. When you were out here alone I missed you so dreadfully and did not really feel satisfied at home no matter how good ma and pa were to me."

"It has been a drastic change for you coming from your sheltered background to the dangers and different living conditions at the fort but you have made the best of it. You are a very special girl."

"That's what I like to hear, dear," she said as she touseled his dark hair. "Now we have to get up and meet the day's problems."

"My love I would like to stay here forever with you," he replied, "but my duties call. We are only a small post but many people depend on us and we have a job to do. Next summer thousands of people will pass through to Utah, Oregon and California and the government has given us the job of protecting them from the Indians. I only hope we can accomplish an almost impossible task."

"You will do your best, I am sure," Caroline said. "I have complete confidence in your ability and courage."

"What more could a man ask," he said, "to be loved by such a desirable, beautiful girl as you are and to have her here with him. I am a lucky man."

"Each day brings new changes," she said, "And meeting them is a challenge to us but we will be equal to the challenge."

Chapter 5

Life at Fort Laramie

Sometimes a pet dog at the fort would disappear and that night an Indian lodge would enjoy dog feast. To think of such a thing made Caroline uneasy for she had grown fond of Ned and Iris's dog Missy and she and Peter had adopted a little black and white terrier which had whined and scratched at their door on a cold autumn night. They had named him Tipsy for he was shaking and unsteady when they took him in but he soon recovered when fed and warmed before the blazing fire in the fireplace. He fast became a regular member of their household.

Some of the men had become friendly with nearby Indians and visited their lodges to try their dog feasts. Some said the meat was tasty. At least it was a change from the salt pork, beans, jerked beef and dried vegetables that the army served at their mess. The vegetables were sent in hard dried bricks to be freshened by boiling in water.

On special holidays like Christmas preparation preceded the occasions. For weeks special food was brought into the fort. Roast pig, roast beef, cold boiled ham, jellies of all kinds, pickles, coffee, tea, dried fruit, cake, mince pie and ice cream. Three long dining tables holding about seventy-five people, the officers and non-coms, and their families dined first and then the rank and file soldiers.

Caroline's and Peter's days revolved around their life at the fort. Caroline had quickly adjusted to the new way of life and her pleasant personality had made her a welcome addition to the fort. Peter had been here long enough to fully realize the gravity of the problems between the Indians and the emigrants. Each day a new incident revealing the difficulties of travel over the trail was brought to his attention. The emigrants had been mislead by dozens of contradictory emigrant guides. They were unsure of what routes were best, what kinds of stock to use, how much food and supplies they would need. The mules were faster but the oxen were more adaptable and easier to manage. Some emigrants had started out with too much heavy useless equipment and only the slightest perception of what lay ahead for them in the west. They had encountered violent lightning and thunder storms, Indians of many tribes, mosquitoes that blackened their bread, lack of grass for their animals and traveling buffalo herds. By the time they reached Fort Laramie some were discouraged and ready to return east. Peter was a great help to many a bewildered and exhausted traveler.

Some of the wagons coming into the fort had different mottoes painted on their covers, "Bound for California or Bust" or "Onward to Oregon" was another. Caroline could only hope that they would get there. The year of 49 had been a bad one for the cholera and now the fall of 50 seemed to be no better. The fort hospital had been filled with patients who were ill or dying of the dread disease. Before nightfall the worried-looking mother who had been getting breakfast for the family that morning was dead and her small child was gravely ill.

The post doctor was kept busy assisting the sick people. Some of the army officers didn't want to help the emigrants and an assistant surgeon refused to give aid to one man who begged for help. The young doctor had sent in his resignation to the army. He had become disillusioned with the conditions at Fort Laramie and wanted to go back east. Peter reminded him of his oath to help the sick and told him as long as he was here he must try to help for many people had died along the trail.

One trail-worn wagon came in with one back wheel wobbling on the axle about a month after Caroline arrived. Its occupants looked worn and ill. The man tied up his oxen in front of the officer's quarters and asked Peter who was just coming down the steps where he could find a blacksmith. He tottered as he walked and Peter could hear a woman and a child crying in the wagon.

"We just barely made it," the man mumbled. "My wife and little girl are ill possibly with cholera. We had to leave our baby boy in a grave along the trail. He was the sweetest little fellow just a year old. It almost killed my wife to see him buried in a rocky grave in so isolated a place east of here. He was our only son. My name is George Gibbs. Would you please help us? We were left behind from the train we came with because we could not keep up with the others. We had such wonderful expectations when we left our home in New York to come west but everything possible went wrong. We joined a wagon train but could not stay with it. One of our oxen died west of Scott's Bluff and we had to replace him at the trader's store there. Buck and Red wouldn't work together at first and being an inexperienced teamster I had to learn to control them. Even the wagon began to have trouble coming down Windlass Hill to Ash Hollow and that really wrecked it up some. We were lucky to make it here to Fort Laramie."

Peter said, "I'm from New York State too. Let me drive you over to the blacksmiths to fix your wagon wheel and then I'll show you where the hotel is located. I'm sure now that you can get a room there. The end of the summer rush will be soon be over and only those who are wintering here are still around. It is too late to start over the mountains. You can see the snow on the Laramie peak up there. The snow falls early in these mountains and stays late in the spring and the winters are bitter cold."

"Indians have been the least of my worries," said George. "Most of our troubles have from my inexperience with traveling

75

and poor equipment. The trader at St. Joseph really took advantage of us."

"You can get all you need at the sutler's store here," Peter said. "He buys all the good equipment and supplies from emigrants. His prices are quite high but he is fair and honest. He is a southern gentleman."

He was interrupted by Mrs. Gibbs and a small child of about three who was still crying. "George," she asked. "Did you get help? Peggy and I are feeling quite sick."

"The lieutenant here is going to drive us to the blacksmiths." George told her, "And then we'll get a room in the hotel. He advises us not to try a trip over the mountains this late in the year."

"Oh dear," Mrs. Gibbs who was a young woman pale and sickly looking, said, "Must we stay in this desolate outpost with such wild-looking Indians around." Just then two Sioux Indians had come by the wagon their faces were painted for war.

Peter reassured her, "There are friendly Indians Mrs. Gibbs. They will not hurt you. The army will protect you here. The nearest trading post is at Fort Bridger and that is a long way away and not nearly as large with a long stretch through an alkali desert and the mountains. My wife is here and several other women so you will not be alone. I can get your husband work when he is feeling better. The army can use civilian workers here to help at the stables and in various other jobs at the fort.

"Thank you," George said as Peter and he climbed up in the wagon. Still shaking he said, "Maybe we should see the doctor first. Betsy has been feeling quite ill since we left Scott's Bluff."

Peter drove the wagon to the office where the doctor saw them and while they were shaken and ill he found they were recovering and with care would soon be better. Peter let them off with their bags at the hotel and then drove their wagon to the blacksmith's where their oxen were unhitched and put in the corral. Just as he drove in the big right back wheel came off and the wagon jolted to the ground.

Karl, the big brawny Swedish blacksmith with a long dark beard left his anvil to speak to Peter.

Lieutenant, you just made it. One more turn and the wheel would have been gone. They were lucky to get into Fort Laramie."

"They may be here all winter Karl, and George will need work until then. Did Jim Thatcher need anyone to help among the stables? The men have just brought in the last wild hay from the farm up the river and he will need some hands to stack it."

"There are always jobs for good workers." Karl answered.

"Give them a few days to get feeling better," Peter said. "In the meantime I'll let George know where to get a job."

Caroline too wished to help the Gibbs family for she felt a

deep sympathy for them in the loss of their only son and the trouble they had had on the trail. She had seen the predicaments that some emigrants had found themselves in on the trip west. She hoped that she and Peter could soon have a baby although she felt it would be hard to raise a child here at Fort Laramie. There were too many dangers in this frontier life so close to Indian problems and an uncertain future. Now she had learned at first hand the difficulties of the emigrants and their problems with the Indians she was aware of just how volatile a situation it was.

The following morning she went over to the hotel to see if she could help them. She introduced herself and Betsy Gibbs who now was rested and feeling better greeted her at the door.

"You are Lieutenant Meade's wife," she said. "We are so grateful for his help. We were at the bottom of the heap last night when he came to our rescue. George has gone to see about a job."

A little girl who was sleepily rubbing her eyes arose from a bed made on two chairs and came to her mother. "This is our little girl, Peggy," Betsy Gibbs said. "We left our little baby boy John back on the trail. It almost killed us to have to bury him out in that lonely spot but we had to do it. There are so many graves along the trail it makes you sad just to see them."

"I know," said Caroline. "I just got here a month ago. I came out on the stage from St. Joseph. We passed many wagon trains on the trail. It is a very hard trip. I don't think a lot of emigrants know beforehand just what they will have to face."

"They only hope," said Betsy, "to find gold at the end of the trail. George wanted to go to California but now it is too late we will have to stay here for the winter. He was so exhausted last night he was shaking with fatigue and Peggy and I were all in too. Our last wagon train left us at Ash Hollow. They were anxious to get through the mountains and we were ill, our one oxen died and our wagon was breaking down. We are from New York originally."

"We are too," said Caroline. "We must have a lot in common."

Caroline could see that Betsy underneath her problems was a strong, intelligent young woman. Now that she had had time to take a bath and brush her hair she was very attractive. Her blonde hair was wound around her head and her bright blue eyes enhanced her face. She had dressed Peggy and started brushing her hair which was blonde like her own. The little girl was fully awake now and responding to her mother's care.

"Mama," she said. "Where is papa?"

"He's gone to find work," Betsy explained. "We have to stay here for awhile dear."

"Thank you for coming over. May I call you Caroline,"

Betsy said. "I will take Peggy down to the dining room to get some breakfast. George and I ate earlier. Last night I felt so ill I couldn't do anything but after a good night's sleep I'm better."

"Good," said Caroline. "It is nice to meet someone from home. There are so few women here permanently. Peter says that several of the wives have been out this summer but they have gone home now."

She walked with Betsy and Peggy downstairs to the dining area where a middle-aged lady greeted them and gave them a table.

"Goodbye," Caroline said. "I'll see you later. I am living in the officer's quarters that long two-story building at the west side of the fort. They are building some small adobe houses and we may be living in one next year."

"Thank you," Betsy said. "Lieutenant Meade and you will never know how much this has done for us. Say goodbye," she said to Peggy.

Peggy was busy slurping up her oatmeal and with a muffled "goodbye" she stopped to smile at Caroline.

Peter and Ned were on the parade ground drilling the soldiers and some of the new recruits were awkward and confused at the strict discipline in their frontier fort. Facing the dangers of Indian attack they had to keep up the daily schedule of marching and arms drill that was proscribed by the presiding officers at the fort. The United States Army Department seemed so distant and unresponsive at times that the officers here were sometimes on their own. They were undermanned and lacked the modern arms necessary to maintain security for themselves and the civilians they were responsible for here. Meanwhile the officers were following orders from Fort Leavenworth and hoping that the Indians would not attack and that the army would send help if needed. Most of their rifles were flintlocks that were hard to wield at short range. The Indians were now arming themselves with rifles and though they were expert with their bows and arrows they still lacked skill with the new arms.

Caroline was waiting for Peter when he returned to their quarters. He told her about the George Gibb's family. "They seem like real nice folks, Carrie darling. They come from New York too. They just had bad advice, bad luck in crossing the plains and they lost their baby boy around Scott's Bluff."

"I know," said Caroline. "I have just been over to the hotel. Mrs. Gibbs, Betsy, is feeling much better this morning and little Peggy is too. George has gone to see about his job so he must be feeling all right."

"Last year the immigrants brought way too much with them," said Peter, "and now some of them run out of food and need equipment at the Fort. So much pork and beans and all kinds of heavy equipment were discarded that the trail on both

78

sides of the fort looked like a junk yard."

"It seems such a waste," Caroline replied. "I hope next year will be a better one for all of them."

Occasionally James Bordeau, a French trader, who had been at Fort Laramie when it was an American Fur Post called Fort William came by with his Brule wife. He was known to be on good terms with the Platte River Sioux and now ran the American Fur post not far from the fort. He was a short stocky man with a round face and mustache and they came riding in on Indian ponies. He could speak in French or broken English articulately but sometimes he was silent and uncommunicative.

The commander welcomed him for he could provide useful information about the Indians, where they were and what their plans were. Usually he kept much of his knowledge to himself for he well knew the Indians desire for privacy and loyalty. He could sense danger instantly when challenged by another Frenchman and taunted by his wife and the opponent to fight or be called a coward he retreated to safety rather than face the consequence.

Some tribes were not welcome at the fort and it was barred in defense. The Crows had ransacked a Sioux cemetery nearby the fort and the traders had watched the orgy of destruction from the parapets. One Indian climbed up a pole and scaled the wall. James Bordeaux had caught him by the neck and pushed him back. Sometimes they only let in a few Indians at a time in the store so they could control the situation. The Indian braves would do anything even to giving their wives and daughters to the "Yellow Hair: for a keg of whiskey. Under its influence they became an uncontrollable mob, running from lodge to lodge, inviting all to drink, whooping, singing, ejecting the liquor from mouth to mouth. The dogs howled at the commotion and it was a scene frightening to the soldiers who had gone to Squaw Town.

One wise Sioux chief warned his people against liquor saying, "Fire water is the redman's enemy." The Crows called it "Fool's water," but still the traders dispensed the watered down liquor which was brought from Mexico and up the Missouri River. It was a sure method of obtaining the furs from the Indians. By the time Peter and Caroline had got to the fort the hey days of the mountain men and fur traders were drawing to a close.

Jim Bridger came to the fort when he travelled east to visit the sutler's store. He then continued on to St. Louis to bring back goods for his new trading post which was farther west on Black's Fork. He and his partner Louis Basquez had opened a post there and had a blacksmith shop and store for supplies. A traveler going east had told Peter about the Bridger post and the beautiful spot where it was located. Here grass and timber and good water were available. The Mormon emigrants had stopped there to repair their wagons and obtain supplies.

James Bridger was a loquacious guest telling of his experiences in the mountains with the Indians. Everyone in the store was fascinated by his stories and his descriptions of the Rocky Mountain country. He had had two Shoshone wives and both had died. His first wife had died in 1846. He had remarried and his second wife had also died at his post. He was enthusiastic about his new venture and its position on a well-traveled trail west. He said he needed supplies and would bring back a wagon load in the spring. His partner Louis Vasquez, a Mexican, was taking care of the post while he was gone. He still loved to travel as in his mountain days and was away from his post a great deal of the time.

Peter said to Caroline, "Jim Bridger was one of the mountaineers in the area and that he had learned much in his travels to the west especially in dealing with the Indians. The department of the Army had hired him as a guide for some expeditions. He is a hardy and energetic man. With all the inexperienced travelers coming west we need such men for advice about the mountains."

Caroline had read of Jim Bridger's exploits in the papers back home where he was regarded by the young boys as a hero. Here he was, Caroline decided a large man with dirty buckskin clothes, a frouseled beard and unprepossessing appearance. It was hard to realize just how much western history had been influenced by this man.

They were constructing new buildings all the time now. Limestone and sandstone had been quarried from the banks of the Platte and hauled up the Laramie to make foundation blocks for the new buildings. A long two-story building was finished to house the bachelor officer's quarters and a string of small adobe houses for the officers with families were being built on the east side of the fort. In the fall Peter and Caroline had seen an infantry company move into temporary quarters in a large new stable and two mounted rifle companies had occupied the new barracks which had been built for only one. It was crowded but the soldiers were glad to get inside after a winter spent in tents in the frigid Wyoming Territory. By December 1850 the single officer's quarters later known as Old Bedlam was almost completed. It still needed pillars and a roof for the porch and balcony. They were still constructing a quarter-master and commissary storehouse, a hospital and adding quarters for officers and enlisted men.

George and Betsy and little Peggy were now settled in at the hotel which was a long log building with rooms at the back and a dance parlor and bar near the front. Here dances were held and the soldiers could dance with the girls, generally the laundresses, who were at the fort. If there were no partners available the men danced with each other and the music was furnished by travellers or teamsters who were staying at the hotel at the time.

George who was a good worker had found plenty to do around the fort. The Gibbs had become good friends with Peter and Caroline and Ned and Iris and Peggy played with little Ned.

"How many emigrants and gold seekers do you think have been past Fort Laramie in the past year?" Peter asked George.

"A great many," George said. "From the looks of the grass along the trail and so many graves."

"The post commander says about 50,000 people have come west last year," Ned said. "No wonder the Indians are restless," said George. "I wouldn't like to see all those people if this was my country."

"The commander is worried about an Indian attack on the fort and has sent a letter to the Commander at Fort Leavenworth saying, "I have to request authority to turn over flintlock muskets and accouterments as soon as possible and percussion muskets and equipment arrive. The fort is not protected by the latest guns." Peter said.

Ned added, "Tom Fitzpatrick, the Indian agent, has gone to St. Louis to tell Colonel David Mitchell that the Indians need compensation for their losses to the emigrants. They have been stealing horses and robbing and harassing emigrants on the trail in retaliation for their loss of buffalo and foliage to the intruding wagon trains. He returned but funds have not been provided and the House of Representatives had killed the bill. I hope they can settle their difficulties before things explode here."

Caroline interrupted, "Let's just enjoy being together. It is only two weeks to Christmas. We have to make it as good as possible. Remember little Ned asked if Santa Claus could get way out here."

"Yes said Iris. "We just received a box from my parents. They wanted to be sure we got it in time and it is hard to know just how long it will take to get out here."

"I'm making a new dress," Caroline said. "for the holiday dance at the sutlers. I've got it cut out. Could I use your sewing machine Iris? Iris got a sewing machine that an emigrant lady left at the fort and she had let me use it," she told Betsy.

"We'll really miss our folks this Christmas," Betsy said, "first year we have been away."

"Me, too" Caroline said. "I'll especially miss little Jed and Harry and the others but I am so happy to be here with Peter." She took his hand and squeezed it.

They talked on exchanging reminiscences and George said, "Betsy, we'd better take Peggy home now. I have to get up early to get my work done at the stables. The horses and mules still have to be fed. Thanks for your dessert Caroline. You can really make a dandy pie. Thank Peter for everything.

He woke Peggy gently and she opened her blue eyes as he wrapped her carefully in a blanket. "Come on dear, he said to Betsy, "Let's get back to our room in the hotel I do some work around the hotel too."

One cold night Peter suggested that they all go skating on the Laramie River and then come back home for coffee and some of Caroline's dried apple pie.

"We don't have skates," George said. "We left them behind when we came west, about the only thing we didn't try to bring," He added ruefully.

"Caroline just skates with her boots. The ice is thick and smooth now. Luckily Ned and I were given some skates by an emigrant who stopped here and wanted to exchange them for a leather belt and some gun powder," said Peter.

Iris said, "We must slide around the edge and let the men do the fancy skating. Maybe the sutler will lend George some skates. He has almost everything at the store."

"Come on," Caroline said. "Let's get a really warm wool coat on and a stocking cap and warm gloves. The wind gets so bitter here and Peggy and little Ned can stay with Bright Star at our quarters until we get back."

The sutler found a men's pair of skates and loaned them to George. Ned and the children came back to Caroline's to stay until their parents returned.

The six friends walked down to the river and there saw many soldiers carrying torches to light up their favorite skating spot.

"Look," said Peter, "the full moon is coming up in the east. We'll soon have light enough to skate.

Caroline replied, "How romantic. It is lighting up the parapets on the fort."

Peter, Ned and George put on their skates and soon were skating out in circles. Caroline and Iris and Betsy were sliding along together for the ice was smooth and strong. Peter was cutting fancy figures as he glided over the ice.

"Show-off," Caroline teased. Then to the girls, "Peter loved to skate at home. He once took a prize for fancy skating."

Iris said, "I wish I had my skates. I used to love to skate but I must be careful now for I am pregnant again. Ned said he would push me around on a chair if I got tired."

Caroline said, "Oh, that is wonderful Iris. Little Ned will have a little brother or sister to play with now. There aren't many children here."

"We can't think about another baby now," Betsy said, "We are still so sad about our little son."

Ned, Peter and George were racing down the river and Ned with his powerful strength reached the set point first. They came back slowly like three shaggy animals in their buffalo robes and fur caps which were the winter apparel for the soldiers.

Ned said, "I've got to give Iris a ride on the chair. She's in the family way, you know."

They approached their wives who were still skating along the river's edge. Peter took Caroline out on the ice, George skated along with Betsy holding on to his arm and Ned helped Iris onto an old oak chair that had been left by the river. They had to skate more slowly now as the group went out on the ice. Ned began singing "My Old Nelly Gray" and they all joined in the song. The other skaters parted as they approached and quite a few, "Hello Lieutenant" and "Hello Sergeant" calls greeted Peter and Ned as they swung around and came back to the starting point.

"Isn't it a lovely night," Betsy said. "It makes me think of skating on the pond at home. To Peter she said, "It must be really nice to have Caroline here now, Peter. I couldn't let George come west without Peggy and I."

"She's my darling," Peter said as he squeezed Caroline around the waist.

"Don't we look like a bunch of lost mountain men? Ned said. "We really have to dress for this winter weather. You women look fairly normal." To Peter he asked, "Aren't we lucky to have our wives with us?"

They enjoyed the moon that was high in the sky now and lighting the willows and cottonwoods along the river.

"I'm getting cold," Said Iris as a slight wind came over the plains.

Ned pushed her into shore and said, "Just one more race down the river and then we'll go home to a cup of coffee warmed with a touch of whiskey and Caroline's delicious apple pie."

The friends returned to Peter and Caroline's quarters where they took off their heavy clothes and gathered around the fireplace. Little Ned and Peggy were asleep on the bed for it was past their bedtime. Bright Star left to return to her lodge outside the fort.

Caroline and Iris cut two big pies into generous pieces and the men hungry after skating eagerly consumed the dessert. The coffee was boiling in the big iron pot and mugs of the strong brew were a welcome drink on a cold night.

Ned and Iris got little Ned up and he said, "Tomorrow is Sunday. We can sleep in awhile and then go to the chapel to hear the chaplain.

George said, "Most of the fort will be in the sutler's store buying liquor and forgetting their problems here in rowdy carousing. No wonder the chaplain is worried about the men."

"Well, said Peter. "Now that Caroline is here I can see why so many of the men are visiting squaw town. It is so lonely and frustrating out here that they are driven to seeking some kind of diversion."

"Me, too." said Ned. "If it wasn't for Iris, little Ned and our coming baby I would be more rambunctious too. I wasn't always the staid family man I am today."

"Come on Sergeant," Iris said, her freckled face glowing from the heat of the fireplace and her present condition well disguised under a ruffled calico dress. "We must be on our way. Little Ned has awakened and is crying."

"We had a great time," Ned said. Next time, Pete, I'll race you farther."

"Fine," said Peter. "I must practice my speed skating."

Peter and Caroline undressed slowly enjoying the warmth of the fireplace. The night would get bitter cold so Peter put another big log on the fire and when Caroline had got into the cold bed he put a big buffalo robe over them.

"Dear," he said. "I'm glad you're not sorry you came. Our friends are really enjoyable to be with aren't they? It was such fun tonight."

She was soon sound asleep now, tired after a strenuous day. Her dark curls were covered with a warm night cap. Her beautiful brown eyes closed but the warmth of her body next to his exuded a feeling of mutual contentment that could not be equaled. What a lucky man he was, he thought.

Bright Star now came every other day keep the quarters clean, take the laundry to the wash room and do other small errands that Caroline needed to have done.

One day Long Lance, her Indian admirer, came to see her while she was at Caroline's. He was dressed in fringed leggings from his ankle to his crotch which were tied with a belt of strips of decorated deerskin and a breech cloth. A deerskin shirt completed his costume and his sleeves were beaded and decorated with porcupine quills. Colorful moccasins covered his feet. His face was vermillion and white and painted for war.

He addressed Bright Star. "Tonight we are going on a raid to get horses from the Crows, our enemies. They have a herd they stole many miles from here. I will see you when I return." His black eyes gleamed fiercely like hard pieces of coal.

Bright Star trembled, "May the Great Spirit protect you Long Lance. Do not steal from the white men on the trail. Do you have your sacred medicine bundle?" she asked.

"White men steal lands and buffalo and grass from red man" Long Lance protested. Why do you like them?"

"They are my friends," she replied. "They are good to me."

"They speak with forked tongue," Long Lance said. "We can not trust them."

Bright Star's eyes filled with tears.

Caroline soon learned about the Indians nearby from Peter

84

and Iris. The Brule were called that because it was the French name for "burned one" and the tribe had once been decimated by a prairie fire. The Sioux had moved west from Minnesota and now were warring with the Arapaho, Blackfoot and Crow tribes. Traders had induced them to make their home here and now there were many lodges that wintered outside Fort Laramie trading with the sutler and getting whiskey and goods for their furs and buffalo robes. The Sioux relied on the buffalo for food, coverings for lodges, saddles, halter, rope, bow strings, clothing, robes and blankets. They used every part of the buffalo for some essential need.

Peter told Caroline one morning that the Oglala, Sioux were going on a buffalo hunt. A herd had been seen only five miles away. The entire village was leaving to take part in the hunt. The squaws and children too were leaving their lodges by the fort. Caleb and Waiting Star were going with them.

Peter said, "Buffalo have poor eyesight but a good sense of smell. The Oglala will have to ride with the wind to have a good hunt. When we were coming out with Colonel Sanderson I tried to shoot one but he got away. It is not easy to bring a big bull down."

One day Peter said, "Twice a year Bull Bear comes in to trade his furs. Sometimes the Brule camp on the North Platte. When they approach they fire their guns and the fort gunners answer with a volley. Some of the Indians get drunk and really insolent and surly and steal any loose articles they can at the sutler's store. Once a trader had to close doors and windows and build a fire to chase out the Indians. They come to get calico, tobacco, whiskey, guns, ammunition, vermillion paints, combs, mirrors, blankets and knives." The chiefs are very generous with their wives and daughters and offering them to the soldiers for a keg of whiskey."

Caroline said, "No wonder some of the soldiers go to Squaw Town. There are so few white girls here for companionship and some of the Indian girls are very pretty. I'm glad I came dear."

"No gladder than I am." Peter responded.

The dust was flying in the air as the whole Sioux camp departed for their hunt. Their tepees were struck, poles taken down and buffalo robes covering removed. The squaws did all the work. Dog and horse travois carried their supplies and papooses.

"The squaws will do the most work." Peter said. They will cut up the buffalo meat, dry it into pemmican, dress the skins and make use of every bit of its carcass, even the tongue and nose are delicious. The chiefs have decided that now is the right time for their hunt."

"Do they have guns?" Caroline asked.

Peter said, "The Cheyennes used spears and bows and arrows

before they got guns from the white men. They ride to the right of the buffalo and aim their spear for the kidneys rather than the heart. They have powerful bows and arrows too."

"Where do they make camp?" Caroline asked.

"The chiefs find a good spot near water with timber for drying scaffolds and a level space for stretching and drying hides close to the buffalo feeding grounds. Sometimes they burn the grass to concentrate the animals in a small area. The hunt leader signals the mounted men and they all rush in on the herd."

"When the men return from the hunt the squaws work begins," said Iris. "They feast on the choice parts of the meat then begin drying the rest."

"Yes," Peter added. "a lodge can take about eleven to twenty-one buffalo hides depending on its size."

"Drying the hides is a big job for the squaws." Iris said. "They have to remove the flesh and gristle and work the hair off until the skin is even in thickness. They mix brains, liver, soapweed and grease and apply it to the hide. Then it is dried overnight and the hide softened by working it over taut sinew or through the hole of a buffalo shoulder blade. Ned explained the process to me."

Caroline said, "It must take much patience and hard work to be an Indian squaw."

Iris said, "They do beautiful beadwork, porcupine quill work on their clothes and moccasins, shirts and smocks. You have seen the colorful work that Bright Star has done."

"It will be good when she has a lodge of her own." Caroline agreed.

Some of the officers in the fort did not want to be useful to the emigrants regarding them as nuisances but the Commander was indignant to hear this and instructed the officers to be helpful to all travelers. "We are in this fort," he said, "to protect American citizens and all others on the trail."

Peter agreed but was torn between his duty as a soldier and his friendship for Caleb and one of the Indians. Caroline tried to help him sort out his feelings and make a compromise without giving up his principles.

"It is hard," he declared one day, "to straddle a fence. I can understand the problems on both sides of this conflict but as a soldier I must obey my commander."

Caroline soon learned to like the life at the fort for she had a basically friendly, understanding personality. Raised in a sheltered New England family she now was placed in a strange environment with a mixture of races with problems unique to her culture. She had learned to cope with the seemingly endless problems at the fort.

She made friends with the sutler and his wife, the Scandinavian and English girls who did the fort's laundry and the endless stream of emigrants who entered the fort's gates. The girls drank too much and became too friendly with the young soldiers at the dances held each Saturday at the sutler's store but Caroline realized that they too had trouble adjusting to a new country and life in a remote fort far from their native land.

Before Ira left she gave him some letters to take back to St. Joseph to be sent east to her parents. She had been astonished to see how Ira had looked at the dance when Peter took her to visit the hotel one Saturday. He was nattily attired in a buckskin suit with fringed and beaded jacket, high heeled decorated boots with leather gloves that matched his jacket. He took part in the square dances, jauntily whirling the girls around and enjoying the rhythm of the fiddle played by one soldier and the jew's harp accompaniment of an emigrant. He had little resemblance to a dirty, dust-covered stage driver she had accompanied west.

Peter remarked to her. They all get a little rowdy on Saturday nights after all they need a little diversion from the everyday problems here."

Everyone was enjoying the social, some drinking to excess and becoming arrogant and unreasonable and others more restrained and amiable.

Caroline saw Henry talking to the sutler trying to sell him some goods. His bald head was shining from the heat of the fireplace where a blazing fire made a part of the big room too warm. It was evident that he had had too many drinks out of his bottle of whiskey on the bar.

"Hello, Caroline, he guzzled, "Is this the famous Peter you've been talking about all during the trip."

Caroline introduced them and said, "Peter, this is Henry. We came out on the same coach so we have become friends."

"Get to know a lot about people on a long trip," Henry said. "You have one sweet little lady for a missus, fellow. Better take good care of her. She is a real trooper. There aren't many girls like her."

"I will," said Peter as he put his arm around Caroline.

Just then Ingrid, one of the laundresses, came to get Henry to join in another square dance.

Peter said to Caroline, "This is Ingrid. She just came from Ft. Leavenworth a few weeks ago. She hasn't been in America long."

Caroline saw that she was a short, sturdy blonde girl with a lovely complexion and bright blue eyes.

"Happy to meet you," she said warmly taking the girl's hand which was red and chapped from working in the laundry.

"Me too," Ingrid said. Your Peter such a goot man. I do not speak much English yet."

She took Henry's hand and led him, tipsy and shaky, to the

group of dancers.

"One thing," Peter said, "there are three Danish girls who can talk with each other and be friends and two who speak English. I'm trying to learn some Spanish from my friend Manuel and some French to communicate with the French traders. There were many Spanish and French people here you know before we came west."

Christmas even here in the far out post of Laramie was an event of importance. Everyone looked forward to its coming and special food was brought in to help celebrate the day. Peter had brought Caroline a cameo brooch at the sutler's store and succeeded in keeping it safe by leaving it with Iris until Christmas Eve. Packages from Peter's father and Caroline's family had been brought from Fort Leavenworth by a special wagon express. The letters enclosed were eagerly read by both and the presents put out around the fireplace to be opened on Christmas morning. Caroline had bought him a special book of poems and a novel.

"My dearest, Her Christmas message read, "I am the happiest woman on earth to be loved by such a dear and sweet husband. I awake each morning to bless the day that I met you and my love is as constant and ever-growing as the sun which comes up each day I spend with you.

Love Always,
Caroline

With his cameo he told her on Christmas Eve just before they left for the Christmas Eve Ball at Old Bedlam, "My dearest, no one could love a wife like I do you. Your beautiful sweet face is in my mind always. For you to join me here is a sacrifice too great for many wives but for you it is just a token of your love." He kissed her passionately.

Oh darling," she said. "Does this new dress look good on me. She had put a pink fabric rose in her dark hair and her big luminous eyes sparkled. She had let little curls fall around her ears to soften her coiffure and made a coronet around her head.

"You are beautiful," he whispered. "I'll have to keep the men in line or they will make off with you.

"Old Bedlam was lighted with numerous kerosene lamps and after getting Ned and Iris and George and Betsy they were greeted by the sound of orchestra music inside. All the officers were in dress uniforms. The commander welcomed the group to the ballroom. The ladies and even the laundresses were gowned in their best attire.

Peter took Caroline's hand and they marched in grand style

around the room after the commander and senior officers and partners. Then the dancing began and Peter and Caroline danced together first. Then they exchanged partners and Caroline found that George was a much smoother dancer but Ned could lead a girl with daring and precision through difficult steps. It was amazing how such a big man could be so light on his feet. He swung her into a spot by Peter as the music ended and said, "She's a good dancer, Pete. Its your turn now." I have to get back to Iris for she's due in a few months and I can't let her dance too much. We're going over to the punch bowl.

Peter who had been dancing gingerly with Iris who was now in the last months of pregnancy led her up to Ned who took his wife's arm and escorted her to the banquet table.

He tasted the pink fruit punch and decided that it had not been doctored with too much liquor yet and Iris could safely drink a glass. Soon Peter and Caroline joined them and the foursome sat on the wooden bench by the refreshment table. George and Betsy had taken their places in a square dance and the caller, a teamster named Bob, was calling the directions for the dancers. An orchestra composed of army musicians, teamsters and even Caleb on his jew's harp kept up a steady rhythmic beat as the night wore on into the late hours. Ned and Iris had left saying that Santa Claus must come for little Ned and they would go home to put out his presents for the next day. Peggy was to stay all night as George and Betsy had left her packages with Ned and Iris.

Peter and Caroline danced together again and then changed dances with the commander and his wife. The commander had admired Caroline's beauty and poise and said, "Caroline you have been a welcome addition to the fort. I wish more of the wives would come out here. The men get restless and unhappy at this frontier post and we have all kinds of trouble with them."

"I can see where they would," Caroline said. "It is a lonely, far-out post to some of the men raised in the east and the conditions are primitive. Then too, we are surrounded by so many hostile Indian tribes. Peter is hoping that Tom Fitzpatrick can arrange a council with the tribes and the army for a peace treaty next year."

"I am too," said the Commander. "We need more communication between the government and the Indians to solve the many problems with the emigrants going west."

The dance was ending and the commander thanked Caroline and Peter swung his superior officer's wife in beside them. "You are a gracious dancer." Peter said gallantly as he bowed to her. She was a thin patrician-looking lady. She had only come out for the holidays and then would return home to Boston.

"Caroline agrees with my hope that next year will bring peace between the surrounding Indians and the army," the commander told Peter. She is a very intelligent girl as well as being beautiful," he added.

"I must agree," said Peter. Caroline, lets say goodbye to the Commander and get back to our quarters. It is Christmas morning now."

"And New Years is not far away," said the commander, "and we must drink a toast to it as the starting point of a New Year of great importance for the peace of this region."

"Right Sir," said Peter as he and Caroline left the brightly lighted hall where some late dancers and musicians were still making merry.

One cold night in the middle of March Caroline and Peter were awakened by a loud pounding on their heavy wooden door. It was Ned in an obvious excited condition holding a reluctant and sleepy little Ned by the hand.

"Pete," he begged, "Could you and Caroline keep little Ned until morning. Iris is having regular labor pains and I am going for the fort doctor. I hope she doesn't have a long labor like she did with little Ned."

The big red-haired Irishman who was so positive and strong in the performance of his army duties was now obviously upset by his concern for Iris and the coming baby. He left quickly slamming the rough hewn wooden door.

Peter took little Ned in his arms and gently laid him on the bed. "There little fellow," he said. "You are going to share my bed tonight. Caroline are you going over to Ned's?" he said as Caroline was removing her nightgown and putting on her clothes.

"I'll see that little Ned is asleep and then I'll go and see if I can help Iris," Caroline replied.

She lay down by little Ned and began singing an old lullaby her mother had sung to her as a child. Little Ned was soon asleep and she got up and softly finished dressing and left their quarters.

Ned had brought the doctor back and Caroline saw that Iris was in great rhythmic pain. The doctor examined here and said, "it will be a while yet."

Ned was pacing back and forth and the doctor said, "Sergeant, calm down and go and get Mrs. Partridge at the hotel. She has been a midwife in the east and can assist me in the birth. Iris is a healthy strong girl and has had a normal pregnancy so all we need is time. He asked Caroline, "Caroline could you get Iris's baby clothes and after Mrs. Partridge cleans him up they will be ready for him." Ned is a typical father and now has to be told what to do."

Caroline found the soft flannel diapers, shirts and nightgowns that Iris had made for the baby and took them from the neat pile in the little dresser. Iris had embroidered little flower patterns around the necks of the gowns and Caroline

90

knew she was hoping for a girl.

Ned soon came back with Mrs. Partridge, a gray-haired motherly looking woman who took charge immediately and got everything in readiness for the birth.

Ned went up to the bed and Iris grabbed his big rough hand and held it tightly.

"Come on my girl," he said. "It won't be long and the pain will be over."

"It's so bad now," Iris moaned.

The doctor checked again and said. "Everything is fine. The cervix is stretching and soon the head will be coming through."

Ned came out in the small outer room where Caroline was waiting.

I thought I wouldn't get so fussed up about it this time," he said. I felt I had learned a lot when little Ned was born but I guess I'm not as tough as I thought.

Caroline said, "Iris is such a special girl always cheerful and courageous. I can see why you are so concerned."

"She's the best," Ned said. "She has made Fort Laramie a bearable place for us to be."

"The doctor says everything is fine," Caroline replied. "The time passes so slow when you are waiting. Bright Star will come in the morning and take care of little Ned if Peter has to go on duty."

"Thank you for helping us out," Ned said. "You and Peter are real friends."

"We are glad to do it," Caroline answered.

They sat and dozed fitfully in their chairs until they were awakened by the loud cry of a baby. The doctor came out and said, "You have a beautiful baby girl, Sergeant, and Iris is doing fine. Just needs a little rest now."

"Sounds like she has good lungs," Ned said and went in to find that Iris, worn and exhausted but happy with her new daughter was resting quietly. "It's a girl," Iris said. "The doctor says she is fine. I'm so glad it is over."

Mrs. Partridge was cleaning up the baby rubbing her with warm oil and dressing her. She placed the squirming little bit of humanity in Ned's arms.

"Well, Sergeant," she said. "She's a mighty pretty little girl for a new born. Now you can quit fidgeting."

Ned looked down at his new baby girl and his face softened. He carried her over and laid her down in Iris's arms.

"You've done it again, little darling," he said. "She's a beauty."

The morning light was just breaking over the eastern bluffs and Caroline came to see the baby, congratulating her parents and explaining "What a lovely baby she is."

Ned was dressing in his uniform, exuberant at his new status as a second-time father and ready to drill the new soldiers on the parade ground. Caroline left a sleepy Iris in the care of Mrs. Partridge and went home to tell Peter and little Ned about the new arrival at the post. Later Ned would come and get his son and take him home to see his new sister.

Iris with her usual resilience was soon taking care of Mary Ellen her new baby and little Ned and Caroline spent many hours helping her with the children. It made their situation at the fort more endurable and their worries about Indian attacks further away.

Chapter 6

The Grand Council of Horse Creek

When Thomas Fitzgerald was appointed Indian agent for the Upper Platte and Arkansas Agency in 1846 he saw the developing problems between the Indians and the white emigrants and settlers. He had the foresight and administrative ability to want to do something about it. "White Head" as he was known by the mountain men and Indians believed that a council among the various Indian tribes and the government representatives could bring some settlement for their difficulties.

After much debate and hesitation the congress in 1851 approved a General Appropriations Act and provided $100,000 to defray the expenses. Fitzpatrick had gone to St. Louis to see David Mitchell, Superintendent of Indian Affairs and then to Washington D. C. with him to promote the idea. When he came home he spent some time visiting the various Indian tribes in the region and urging them to come to a council which was to be held at Fort Laramie. The commanding officer and other officers including Peter and Ned thought it would be a good idea and although they knew of the hostility between various tribes and the possibility of trouble among them they welcomed a chance to ease the tension between the redmen and their own government and people.

Fitzgerald held meetings with the Cheyenne, Arapaho, Comanches and Kiowas. The Apaches refused to travel so far. He sent messengers to all the northern tribes, Oglala, Brule, Crow, Gros Ventres, Mondan, Arikara and other Sioux tribes. Major John A. Holeman who was the newly appointed agent of the Indians of Utah Territory succeeding Brigham Young wanted to include his wards in the council. He was eager, energetic man anxious to make a name for himself in settling the Indian's problems. He hurried to talk to the Snake or Shoshone chiefs who decked in feathered finery rode east with him. The Snakes were old enemies of the Sioux and Fitzpatrick and the army officers were apprehensive lest trouble be caused by the arrival of the Snakes.

In the summer of 1851 the Indians began to assemble at the fort with the nearest tribes coming first. Peter and Caroline were astonished at how many Indians were coming. With their squaws and papooses and dog travois carrying supplies and their horses the fort was surrounded by the lodges of the redmen.

"Peter," Caroline said, "I only hope this does not result in further trouble. It makes me nervous to see our small army in the fort outnumbered by so many Indians."

Peter replied, "Yes and Major John Holeman, the newly appointed agent of the Utah Territory wants to include the Snake or Shoshones. He wants to leave tomorrow to have a council with them. He is a very energetic man.

Caroline asked, "But aren't the Snakes the enemies of the Sioux and Crows and didn't they desecrate the Sioux burial ground near the fort? Bright Star says they are always fighting. The Snakes will hate to pitch their tepees next to their bitter foes."

"We will have to wait and see," Peter cautioned. "Maybe they won't come."

Sixty Snake chiefs and delegates decided to ride east with Major Holeman and though the Cheyenne attacked them and killed two Snakes they still came on to Laramie. The Fort Laramie commander sent out a small detachment with Peter leading them to meet the Snake delegation. Included in the group of soldiers were four musicians hoping to forestall any trouble with the tribes. As the Snakes approached, the bugler was ordered to play "Boots and Saddles." The sound of the music seemed to quiet the Snake warriors and they came on without any problem. All activity in the Sioux camp stopped. All of them came running to see their enemies and the Sioux women who had lost loved ones in Snake attacks were moaning and crying. On came the Snakes moving to a stream closer than a mile from the Sioux. Peter and his men, the interpreters and the fort personnel watched nervously at their approach. A Sioux brave rode straight toward a Snake chief. The latter halted and gave a savage battle cry. One of the French interpreters fearing the worst raced after the Sioux warrior. The Snake chief was walking his horse and aimed his rifle but the interpreter yanked the Sioux warrior from his horse halting the trouble. Thus an incident which might have had a serious consequence was avoided and the council saved.

Peter invited the Snakes to camp next to the army troopers to keep them separated from the rest of the Indians. The commander complimented Peter for his restraint and handling of the situation.

Caroline and Iris waited in the officer's quarters for their husbands return. They were anxious for the safety of little Ned and Iris's new baby girl Mary Ellen and the position of Peter and Ned in such a highly volatile situation, with so many Indian participants with long and bitter relationships.

Caroline said. "Doesn't it make you nervous to see so many Indians of enemy tribes surrounding the fort?"

Iris with her usual complàisance and good humor said, "Ned doesn't think they can stay here for too long. Their hundreds of animals are using up the grass and food very fast. They may have to find a better place for the council."

Colonel David Mitchell with his group of government and civilian observers was moving west from Fort Leavenworth to attend the council. Before he left St. Louis in July he arranged for a wagon train to carry the gifts for the Indians to be loaded from steamboats on the Missouri. But as in most cases of government planning they were late and were just being packed when he was ready to come. He was very angry for he knew that without the presents no one would have any influence on the Indians or get them to participate in a general council. The effect that the late arrival would have when many were already gathering at Laramie could spell disaster for the plan. At the end of August Peter and Caroline saw Mitchell's group ride into the fort. They were glad that the council would soon take place for the Indians around the fort were getting restless.

Jim Bridger had been chosen to act as an interpreter for the Snake tribe and he arrived at the fort. He had had Shoshone wives and wanted to support the Snakes against the Sioux.

Throughout the first night the soldiers under Peter kept a constant vigil to see there was no trouble. Caroline slept fitfully in the big wooden bed hoping that there would be no fights among the Indians and that Peter would be safe. From the corner posts of the fort that night on every half hour the guard called out the time and "All is well." The Snakes had posted their own warriors on every hill and they were posed with their own weapons in readiness for any emergency. They had been assured by Mr. Holeman and the soldiers that they would be safe but they wanted to be sure.

For three days Colonel Mitchell delayed the council waiting for the distant delegations of Indian tribes. The Assinboines from Fort Union with Major Culbertson and Father De Smet had many hundreds of miles travel through uncharted wilderness to get to Fort Laramie. They had left on July 31, 1851 to cross Montana and Wyoming over hard and desolate country. There were thirty-two people in the group. Their destination was eight hundred miles from their home. They took two four-wheeled wagons and two carts for transportation of provisions and baggage.

They spent two days up the valley of the Yellowstone and eleven days to Fort Alexander on the mouth of the Rosebud River. The swarms of mosquitoes in this hot month of the year were so annoying that they had to wear sacks over their heads. They waited seven days for their other effects to be brought down the river in a barge. They ferried to the south bank of the Yellowstone River where poor water was a part of their trials. They then crossed the rugged terrain of the Tongue River where they found good water and along the eastern base of the big Horn Mountains. They found a lake and named it after Father De Smet. They crossed the valley of the Powder River where frequent gullies and desert caused the teamsters trouble. They had not arrived when the council had decided to move to Horse Creek. They joined the Oregon Trail one hundred-sixty miles

95

west of Laramie and had to double back to the Fort only to learn that the council had been moved to Horse Creek thirty-five miles farther east. It was an exhausted group of travelers who arrived at the fort to learn at the sutler's store that the place for the council had been changed.

Colonel Mitchell was still unhappy over the delay of the wagons bringing gifts for word that with the late start in getting them sent it would be two weeks before they crossed the Laramie. The grass on the creek above the fork was almost gone and the Indians were getting restless. The officers agreed that it would be wise to move to Horse Creek which was only thirty-five miles away on the North Platte and two days nearer for the army train.

Caroline was delighted to hear that the council was moving for the dust created by the Indians, the yelping of dogs and the confusion and danger were beginning to wear on everyone in the fort. Peter had told Caroline to stay close to the officer's quarters for with so many Indians coming into the fort no one was safe until the council was over.

Peter came into their quarters to pack for the trip. We are taking three troops of cavalry and one of infantry," he said. "There will be only a skeleton crew here at the fort. Don't worry Caroline, I will be back and I hope some of our problems are settled there. Damn that wagon train for being late. I hope it doesn't wreck Colonel Mitchell's chances for peace. He is very upset about it."

"I will pray for you and all the men and hope this uncertainty is soon ended." Caroline replied.

"Darling," he said. "You give me courage. Remember always how much I love you."

He kissed her ardently and she responded as though their separation was for a long time.

Caroline and Peter arose early the day of the move to Horse Creek. The sounds of army wagons, the clattering of cavalry horses, the shouting of the officers and men as well as the yelling of the Indians, the yelping of dogs and the general confusions of Indian entourage made it impossible to sleep. No one in the fort was unaware of the event.

The grass near Fort Laramie at this time of year was depleted by the many emigrant wagons who had passed by and had to feed their cattle and other animals on the foliage along the trail. The wild hay that the soldiers had cut and stacked for the fort would not have lasted long for this immense encampment and would mean that the army animals would go hungry in the coming winter. Clouds of dust had arisen with each arrival at the fort and the mixture of unfriendly tribes could be explosive if the Indians had obtained liquor. Caroline feared for Peter's safety for the Indians outnumbered the whites over 30 to 1.

As Peter was drinking his coffee that Caroline had made they heard a knock at their door. Ned called, "Are you ready Pete. We must be mounted to lead the cavalcade to Horse Creek."

"Right away Sarge," Peter answered. He put on his coat and hugged and kissed Caroline hurriedly. She cautioned him, "Please be careful dear, some of the young braves are looking for trouble and only the wise old chiefs are trying for peace. Bright Star is worried about the Snake Indians. They are old enemies of her people and Long Lance told her he will not let them go in peace for they killed his father."

Peter replied, "It is a chance for peace and we must take it. Old Fitz thinks we have a chance now and I only hope he is right. He is an expert of Indian life and an experienced mountain man."

Iris Delaney came up just then and the two young women went inside to get another cup of coffee and discuss the problems of the day.

"Iris," Caroline asked of her friend whose toweled red curly hair hung around her shoulders. "How have you remained so calm when Ned has to go with the army on such a dangerous detail. I worry dreadfully about Peter's safety."

"Well," Iris replied. Ned is such a big rough Irishman that he can handle himself in any situation. He has had several fights with drunken Indians and he has handled them easily. They respect him for his honesty and his strength. The Sioux call him Yellow Hair with the Strong Arms."

"Peter is so gentle and kind," Caroline said. "He is strong but seldom shows his boxing prowess. He wants so much to see the government settle peacably with the Indians and end this hostility. I hope they come to some understanding at this council. The government may not get the wagons with the goods for the Indians here in time."

"Ned has no illusions about what the government will give the Indians, Iris said. "Most of the wagons are loaded with things the Indians cannot or won't use. I only hope that all the tribes can live peacably together for a few days."

"The Indians have many complaints," said Caroline. "The buffalo are getting scarcer now and the trail cut through their lands have widened. Thousands of easterners and foreigners lured by California gold and the opening of new lands in the west are making their way across the prairies and to the mountains of Wyoming. Buffalo are the Indian's indispensable source of food, clothing and lodging. They have to ride far south from their natural hunting ground to find the buffalo. There were two vast buffalo herds so huge they filled a whole valley back to back and once roamed the prairies one north and one south of the Platte. Now the herds are fewer north of the river and the white men are killing more of them each year and the Indians are getting hungry. I can't blame them for being upset.

Just then Bright Star knocked on the door. She had come to tell Iris that little Mary Ellen was crying like she had the colic. She had brought little Ned with her. Iris said, "I'll go right down and you stay and help Caroline with her work. Caroline asked Bright Star, "Do you think there is any chance for peace with all the tribes?"

The little Indian girl said softly, "Many tribes, many hate each other Snakes and Blackfoot and Crows, bad Indians. Great Father in Washington must send food soon. Buffalo have been gone long time, riders go far to hunt them. Many of my people are hungry and the cold winter will be coming soon. Snow will soon be whitening the mountains."

"There are so few of our men," Caroline replied. "I will be glad when the council is over and Peter is back in the fort."

"I'm sure Ned will be all right," Iris said. I just can't think anything else now. Our baby will be six months old soon and Ned has promised to build me a new crib for her." She took little Ned by the hand and they went back to their quarters.

Bright Star made the bed, washed the dishes and swept the sand from the floor. Iris told Caroline as she left. "Don't worry all the time. I feel it in my bones that they will be safe. You can't stand it here if you worry all the time. I'm piecing a new quilt for my baby for her new bed. If you keep busy the time will soon pass. It will only be a few days and Ned says a rider will bring us the news as soon as an agreement is reached."

It was a miserable time of year for such a big encampment to move. The September days were hot and sultry and the dust followed the train which was several miles long. Both Indian horses and dogs pulled travois of tent poles loaded with buffalo robes, cooking ware, children and small dogs. The Indian women with characteristic stoicism had broken camp and some of them had wisely made a canopy over the travois. Ahead of the Indian cavalcade rode the uniformed soldiers. Peter was riding his favorite horse Diamond and Ned was on Big Red. The more rambunctious Indian braves were making the trip miserable by riding at full speed alongside the soldiers and stirring up the dust of the road and letting out warwhoops as they came. Peter said to Ned, "Those beggars are really making it a miserable trip but we cannot challenge them or it may lead to a fight." They arrived at Horse Creek on September 5th and Colonel Mitchell assigned camping spots to the various tribes. Through the 6th the Indians were still arriving and the Crows and Assiniboines and northern Indians had not yet appeared. Mitchell to prevent trouble assigned the Snakes a place east of the creek with the stream and a company of soldiers with Peter and Ned between them and their traditional enemies.

All night the Snake Indians had their sentinels posted on every important knoll and a warrior wrapped in a blanket kept a constant vigil for they did not trust their enemies, the Sioux. Jim Bridger who was their interpreters told the officers, "Uncle Sam told them to come here and they would be safe but they ain't taking his word for it altogether." There were three troops of cavalry and one of infantry here at Horse Creek, but with about 10,000 Indians and about 300 white soldiers, officials and civilians there was cause for worry.

The next day was Sunday and Colonel Mitchell announced that this was the white man's medicine day on which no business could be conducted. The squaws were busy all day laying out a conference ground and erecting willow shelters for shading the Indians from the hot autumn sun and an arbor for the white dignitaries. The Sioux in the evening staged dog feasts and dancing and singing and accompanied this with incessant drum beats and war whoops. There was little sleep for anyone at the council.

All night the soldiers were on the alert and every half hour came call Number 2, 12 o'clock, all is well. Peter and Ned slept with their heads resting on their saddles covered with a blanket for the nights were getting cold. They slept fitfully as any movement of the horses or men could signal the start of trouble. They were glad when day light broke and the night ended. Several hundred mounted braves had insisted on riding with them to Horse Creek and they wondered how much trouble they would make here at the council.

The Sioux according to their custom staged dog feasts for the Cheyenne and Arapahos and even for the Snakes who did not eat dogs. They selected the fattest dogs, killed, cleaned and singed them and cooked them until tender in big kettles. Even Father De Smet said it was good meat and tasted like pork.

With the dog feasts there was dancing and singing accompanied by a steady drumbeat and whooping all night. The troops were restless and uneasy but the nights passed without incident. Peter and Ned kept their pistols in their holsters and their rifles beside them for protection against any outburst. Diamond kept whinnying at the din in the Indian camps and Peter went to the grassy spot where the horses were hobbled and patted his horse. "Old Boy," he said. "This won't last too long and then we will be back with Caroline and she can give you a lump of sugar." The big black horse seemed to be reassured at Peter's presence and stopped his restless pacing and whinnying.

Ned had fallen asleep as Peter left. His curly red head the only thing not covered by the bright Indian blanket.

At 9 a.m. the 8th of September the booming of a cannon roused the encampment to summon them to the council. Immediately there was a great procession to the council ground.

The chiefs led the way followed by the braves and finally the women and children. They were attired in their most colorful and finest clothes and even the children wore skins, beads and colored cloth which was trimmed with porcupine quills.

Each tribe contributed their own song to the discordant sounds of the morning. They took their places in a big circle with the western side a third open. The wife of an officer at the fort entered the circle and sat in an assigned seat under the arbor. She was the only white woman there.

The Cheyenne and Snake Indians in a ritual sought peace with each other and the orations by the leading members of the tribes were followed by a feast of boiled corn. The Cheyenne placed gifts before the brothers of men killed on route to the council, the Snakes, and offered them the scalps of the slain men. The children who were orphaned by the killing were exchanged for adoption. Further orations and peace and good will was pledged. The following evening the Cheyenne visited the Snakes at their lodges and danced and sang all night.

The Crows, old enemies of the Sioux and Cheyenne still had not appeared but Mitchell knew he must proceed with the council. Mitchell, Fitzpatrick, Major Holeman, Robert Campbell one of the former owners of Fort William, Father Pierre Jean de Smet, the well-known Catholic priest, the Commander of Fort Laramie, Peter and other officers were in the center of the gathering. Peter was amazed at the huge crowd of Indians that had gathered here on the creek. Surely, he thought some good must come from this council.

Colonel Mitchell brought out a three foot red stone pipe decorated and filled with a mixture of tobacco and kinnykinick. He and Fitzpatrick took the first puffs and then passed it to the Sioux chiefs. The pipe was unwieldy so often the interpreter had to hold the bowl. Many of the smokers would point the pipe in four directions, lift it skyward to the Great Spirit and hold it down to recognize the "bad spirit." After each tribe's leaders had smoked it was refilled and passed on to the next tribe.

Mitchell recognized the wife of the commander of the Fort and said, "In her presence the white men give you evidence of their peaceful intentions.

Peter admired the commander's wife and all the wives who had come out here to be with their husbands. The commander's wife like Caroline had made a big contribution to the life at the fort. The men had behaved better and kept themselves in better condition since the women had come.

A Cheyenne created an incident when she led a pony carrying a young boy into the midst of the council. One of the Snake chiefs had killed her husband and orphaned her boy. She was asking him to adopt her boy. The Cheyenne chiefs stopped her and led them away. Another possible troublesome confrontation had been averted.

The pipe was smoked all around and Mitchell spoke slowly a sentence at a time to be interpreted so they would understand his message. He explained that the Great Father in Washington understood all their problems and would compensate them for their losses to the white men. He asked them to stop warring with each other, agree on boundaries for the tribes and elect one chief with whom the government could transact all their business. The Great Father he said, "Will give you $50,000 for 50 years in goods, merchandise and provisions if you agree to the treaty. If the tribe warred on another and did bad things or injured white immigrants the grant would be taken away.

Mitchell could only promise that the gift train would be here in a few days. He asked them to consider his offer and return the day after tomorrow with their answer. The cannon would be fired and the flag raised as a signal for the meeting.

Fitzpatrick spoke next and urged the tribes to accept Mitchell's proposal. Several chiefs beginning with the Brule, Sioux spoke and said they would discuss the suggestion with their people.

Thus was a whole people intimidated and made inferior by the promises that could not be kept. The redman was beginning to see the end of an era of freedom and personal control of his environment. They were hungry because of the lack of buffalo and believed the white people to be rich, numerous and powerful.

Peter and Ned made sure their horses had grass and watched as the Indian ceremonies continued. Both men were anxious to see the whole affair over and some agreement made. They slept intermittently as guards kept watch during the night. One company of cavalry had had to move their horses to better grass nearby. Peter was impressed by the friendliness of the different tribes now. He could see how the large dog population being depleted in feasts for the buffalo were gone from the vicinity. The commissary wagons kept a good supply of food for the soldiers.

Finally the Crows who were the traditional enemies of the Sioux and Cheyenne began arriving. They had had to come from the Powder River country which was farther away. They rode in like a military column with feather headdresses and showing their weapons and chanting Crow songs. All the encampment admired their appearance and the tribes again smoked a peace pipe.

Colonel Mitchell opened the second session and asked what the chiefs had decided. Once again the Brule Chief spoke first then the others. Some questioned the late arrival of the gift train and asked when they would see the presents they were promised and some seemed ready to agree to the whitemen's terms.

Mitchell and Fitzpatrick were furious at the late arrival of the wagon but they met with the leaders to make a map for the boundaries for the tribes. On the 12th of September they met with interpreters and representatives of each group and with the help of Father De Smet and Jim Bridger drew up maps. The Sioux still insisted on the right to hunt below the North Platte in Cheyenne and Arapaho territory and finally that was agreed upon by all.

Each tribe selected a representative to deal with the government except the many bands of Sioux. Finally Mitchell picked his own choice, a chief of the Wazhazha branch of the Brule band called "Scattering Bear" or simply, "the Bear." The Bear protested loudly for it would be hard to represent the various groups. Mitchell put him in a circle of twenty-four Sioux braves. He gave each a stick and said if they wished to choose the Bear as chief to show it with this stick. After negotiations with the tribe members two came forward to place the stick in the Bear's hand and all the others followed. Then he was chosen as the Sioux representative to negotiate the treaty.

The big encampment of thousands of Indians and hundreds of white soldiers and civilians began to decimate the vicinity of Horse Creek. Sanitary conditions and the dust of early September made conditions intolerable. The soldiers under Peter were complaining of the horrible smell and the unsanitary conditions of the camp. Colonel Mitchell despite his discomfort stayed with his Indian guests.

By the 17th of September Mitchell and Fitzpatrick and the Indian chief had agreed on a treaty. In council, slowly, with interpreters explaining, Mitchell read the treaty. Then Mitchell and Fitzpatrick signed for the United States Government and agreed to protect the Indians from the depredations of the whites. All the Indian chiefs signed with an xx. But Mitchell would not let the Snakes sign and Agent Holeman was upset. Mitchell may have been angry because the inclusion of Snakes in the council had caused many anxious moments for the agent during the council. They were not in his sphere of influence.

Late in the evening of the 29th the wagon train arrived and pulled into the circle. A large crowd of eager Indians gathered around the train. Next day they came dressed in their finest attire to receive the immense pile of goods. Each chief received a general's uniform fit out with epaulettes and sabers which were presented in Mitchell's tent. The boots were too stiff for them and they kept on their moccasins. A certificate of President Millard Fillmore further added to their decorations. The other side of the medal showed clasped hands meaning peace and mutual trust.

The other warriors were given uniforms befitting their station, in the tribe. Brigadiers, colonels and other officers. Gifts of tobacco, cloth, beads, kettles, knives, paints, blankets and various food stuffs were then distributed. For two days the presents were presented and then on September 23rd the encampment began to depart. They had learned that a buffalo herd had been seen on the South Platte. Many of the braves turned southeast for the three days ride.

Many of the goods given to the Indians were left at the encampment, soda and flour whitened the ground. Cotton cloth, thread and bed tickings seemed of no use to squaws used to making clothing of tanned skins. The heavy copper kettles were stacked in piles and remained behind because they were too heavy to carry on the travois.

Ned and Peter seeing the waste of good material and food that Iris and Caroline could have used wondered just why such goods had been brought here. Someone with little understanding of Indian life must have arranged for the gifts. Bolts of cloth had been reeled out by rampaging braves and left to rot on the campground.

It had been the largest Indian council ever held and Father De Smet and Colonel Mitchell were pleased with the treaty and hoped for peace and future good relationships between the white and the redman.

Peter and Ned as they prepared to leave were not so sure. They felt that the sight of so many Indians in army uniforms was ludicrous and that the discarded gifts were a sign of the white man's lack of understanding of the Indian needs. Still they were officers and must return with their men to Fort Laramie. They would be glad to get back to Iris and Caroline.

Kurz, the Swiss artist, who was staying at Fort Union as a clerk said, "The news from Fort Laramie fails utterly to justify the expectation. The U. S. agent Colonel Mitchell is said to be befuddled most of the time by too much drink to have made great promises to the Indians and to have appointed several braves to the rank of supreme chief without approval of the respective nations and Mr. Culbertson has been named a colonel. Colonel of what? Here we have neither regular army or militia."

Culbertson and the Assinboines returned to Fort Union at the headquarters of the Missouri from the council on the 31st of October, 1851. Now would come the days when the army at Fort Laramie and all the participants in this great council would see if anything of value would come from this meeting.

Soldiers from Fort Laramie stayed until all the Indians had gone, the teamsters had taken the empty wagons back to Fort Leavenworth and all the dignitaries had left then the commander ordered them back to the fort.

It was a two day ride back and Peter said to Ned after they had saddled their horses, "Ned, I can't wait to get back to Caroline and you must be anxious to get back to Iris, little Ned and Mary Ellen. It hasn't been a pleasant assignment at the council but I hope it will turn out as well as Col. Mitchell seemed to think."

Ned answered, "Sure and begorra I will be glad to get back to my family and leave this smelly camp behind. I only hope something has been accomplished by our trip here. Some of those young braves are still looking for trouble. You could see how they wanted to anger us when they went riding beside us and kicking up the dust when we were coming here. I hope the wise chiefs will be able to keep them under control. I was afraid one of the new recruits might get spooked and shoot one of those rampaging redmen." "We were very lucky Peter replied, "that none of the possible clashes led to any trouble. Some of the tribes have been bitter enemies for years. It was remarkable that they all cooperated and agreed on boundaries and reparation."

"They are hungry, Ned said, "and they need food for their winter lodges not general's uniforms and medals. I only hope that this peace truce holds."

"I hope their hunters are lucky in their buffalo hunts to the south," Peter said. Most of the young bucks rode out in a hurry when they learned that a herd of buffalo had been seen farther south."

Ned swung up on Big Red and called to the men under his command, "We're going back to the fort now so get in line."

Peter mounted Diamond and rode in behind the commander of the fort. He had sent his wife back in a wagon driven by an civilian fort employee and accompanied by several soldiers. Her courage in coming to such a council had inspired the whole troop of soldiers Peter thought. He would like to tell Caroline about her visit to the camp.

As they rode back and made a camp along the trail Peter said to Ned, "The nights are getting cold now. I will be glad we will be back at the fort tomorrow."

The men quickly pitched their tents that night and went inside. Huge fires would be needed to get some comfort in the brisk September chill. Tomorrow they would arrive at the fort with news about the council.

Chapter 7

Tragedy for Lieutenant Grattan

The year of 1854 would bring new problems and a tragic occurrence near Fort Laramie, the massacre of twenty-eight soldiers and their leader Lieutenant Grattan by the Sioux Indians. The provisions of the peace council had not been approved by the Congress of the United States and so annuities had not been sent to the Indians in time to prevent them from harassing the emigrants traveling west.

Peter had welcomed the arrival of Lieutenant Grattan and the other soldiers with him as a needed addition to the fort. Grattan was a young Irishman, a graduate of West Point. He had been born in Vermont and given an appointment to the academy from New Hampshire. He had received a brevet commission to wait for a vacancy in the regular army. Peter felt that they should have much in common with their mutual background but he found Grattan to be a young man with ambitions to succeed in the military at all costs. He was regarded in the fort as a young officer of much promise, full of military enthusiasm with undoubted daring and gallantry. He was enthusiastic about Fleming's foray and begged the commander to put him in charge of the next expedition.

By others he was regarded as lacking in experience and knowledge of western problems and the feelings of the Indians. He thought they had been handled too mildly for their attacks on the emigrants and boasted that with thirty men he could whop all the Indians on the prairie." On many occasions he tantalized the Indians at the fort and shook his fist at them. One trader observed that he hoped that Grattan could come out safe in a skirmish with the Indians but he doubted it.

The problems between the Indians and the emigrants were getting more severe and only a handful of men at the fort stood between them. The friendly Indians around the fort warned the soldiers that some of their younger tribesmen were just waiting to get revenge against the travellers.

The Miniconjou Sioux had come down from the Black Hills to join the Oglala and Brule who were camped near Fort Laramie. They had never traded with the fur companies in this area and so had no friendship for them. They soon began to harass the emigrant trains demanding gifts. They camped on the north bank of the Platte River near the mouth of the Laramie and formed a village of eighty to one hundred lodges. In mid-June of 1853 they had seized an emigrant and stamped on his papers. They had forcibly seized the Platte ferry boat from its owner. On the 15th a sergeant from the fort had to take the boat from them to cross the river. When he was midstream a

Miniconjou shot at him with a rifle. Fortunately the ball did not hit the boat but fell into the water. The sergeant was furious and had hurried back to the fort to report the incident. Ned saw him riding in and asked, "What has happened?" The sergeant jumped off his horse without answering and hurried into the commander's office to report the incident. Commander 1st Lieutenant R. B. Garnett, a confederate officer who despised the Indians called all his officers together and ordered 2nd Lieutenant Hugh Fleming to proceed to the village and demand that the Indian who had shot at the sergeant be given up to them. Fleming had only graduated from West Point the year before and was a brevet second lieutenant waiting to be assigned a regular commission. He had been here less than a year. Most of the garrison were out with the cattle herd or doing other duties so he led twenty-three enlisted men, the post surgeon and a post interpreter, Auguste Lucien on a march to the Indian camp.

They crossed the Platte in two small boats which made it necessary to make several trips. At the Miniconjou village Fleming halted his men and told Lucien to go to the lodge of the chief, Little Bear. Lucien was told to tell the chief that the culprit who shot at the sergeant was to be given up and the chief too was to be a prisoner for the depradations of his tribe. This was not the Indian way of dispensing justice. Each tribe took care of their own punishment after a meeting of the leaders in council. Lucien found that the chief was not in his lodge. He reported back to Fleming that the chief was not there and then returned to the village and spoke to a group of Indians demanding the offender or other prisoners. They refused to give up any of their men.

Lieutenant Fleming then called the sergeant who had been shot at by the ferry and four other men out of the ranks. He ordered the rest to form a circle for protection against the mounted Indians and then with his detachment marched into the village.

The approach of the soldiers led the agitated Miniconjou to retreat to a ravine at the back of the village. They began shooting at the soldiers with guns and bows and arrows. Fleming and his men returned their attack and drove them away.

There were only about thirty shots fired by both sides but the darkness kept losses at a minimum and only three Indians were killed. Fleming took two Indians prisoners and held inside a hollow square of guards they were taken back to the fort. At dawn he returned to Fort Laramie saying his men had behaved bravely and were a credit to his regiment.

Peter had tossed about fitfully all night and neither he nor Caroline had had much rest. He was glad to hear the approach of the detachment near dawn for he feared the Indians would be hostile to anyone coming into their camp to take prisoners.

Caroline, sleepy-eyed and with her long dark hair uncombed made a big pot of coffee over the fireplace and poured a large tin cup full for Peter. He pulled on his army uniform, washed his face at the washstand, brushed his hair and shaved with a straight razor after sharpening it on a leather strop.

"I feel like raising a beard," he said. I had one before you came and it would be much easier and most of the men have them. I might at least grow a mustache. Don't you think it would be more distinguished, dear?"

"I like you clean shaven," Caroline said, "But you do as you want to. Iris says Ned's beard is so prickly she never enjoys his kisses. But more important did you hear the detachment coming in at dawn. I hope everything went well for Hugh and that there are no casualties on either side."

"Hugh is inexperienced in Indian country," Peter said, "and Caleb says the redmen are in no mood to compromise. Tom has found that he could get the approval of the Arapaho and Cheyenne to the new terms asked by congress but the Sioux are in a starving state and are in want half of the year. The buffalo are fast disappearing and the emigrants are driving them into narrow paths where competing tribes give them trouble. Their women are hungry and the children are crying. Their warriors want revenge. Their promised annuities have not arrived and the government has changed the promises of the Ground Council. They have many grievances."

"It is a difficult situation," Caroline said. I saw Lieutenant Grattan kick an Indian out of his way in the sutler's store. These new officers the army has sent out do not seem to understand the problems of the Indians."

"Some of the Sioux do hang around and make nuisances of themselves." Peter said, "and the white men add to their troubles by giving them liquor for their furs. I have to meet with the officers at the Commanders to hear just what happened at the Miniconjou village. I hope Hugh used good judgment in dealing with them."

The Miniconjou after the Fleming foray and fearful of further attacks began to strike their lodges and move north to the Black Hills. From Fort Laramie a message was sent north asking Chief Little Brave to bring as many of his braves as he could and come back to meet with the commander at the fort. In a few days the chief rode up with about sixty of his warriors. Twenty of them met with Lieutenant Garnett. The commanding officer tried to explain the Fleming attack saying he regretted that any of their people were killed and that they could be friends if they behaved but he warned them against any more attacks on white men.

Little Brave said, "You have done what you thought was right. We wish to live and be friends." Then he asked for a gift to seal their bargain but Garnett refused saying, "If you show by your future conduct that your promises are sincere it will be time to speak of such matters."

Garnett then let the two prisoners go and the Miniconjou departed. He later talked with "the Bear" the Brule chief whom David Mitchell had made the chief of all the Platte Sioux at the Grant Council two years before. "The Bear" said that all the remaining Sioux were friendly. Still the incident rankled in all the Sioux camps and many of the Miniconjou were still angry.

Three months later Thomas Fitzpatrick arrived at Fort Laramie to give the Sioux their annuity goods and to explain to them the way Congress had changed their treaty. He found the Indians in a revengeful mood and requested a troop of soldiers be sent to the camp adjacent to the council. They interrupted his discussion with frequent accounts of their dissatisfaction with the Laramie fort and its soldiers and asked that the fort be removed. "When it was placed here." they said. "We were told it was for our protection but the soldiers of the Great Father were the first to bloody the ground."

One or two chiefs refused to make other treaties but Lieutenant Garnett came from the fort to explain the reasons for Fleming's intrusion into the Indian village. This seemed to quiet them and the chiefs signed the new treaty. Fitzpatrick then distributed their annuities and left the fort.

Peter came into their quarters after returning with the troops and said to Caroline who was embroidering a pillow case, "We are lucky that the chiefs of the Miniconjou accepted Tom's explanation of Fleming's action and the failure of the Congress to live up to the promises that Colonel Mitchell made at Horse Creek. At first they were very angry and disturbed. I didn't know for a while if another skirmish would break out. Both Ned and I alerted our men to possible trouble but we were both grateful that no further fights occurred. The government takes so long in providing for the terms of the treaties and then cuts them way below the original offer. I hope this will settle the problems for a while."

Caroline answered, "Bright Star was very upset. She said one of her cousins were killed by Fleming's attack and her aunt was weeping and moaning all day after he was killed. They do not understand the white man's ways. They are so different from their own."

"Sometimes I can't understand them myself." Pete said. "but I am here to try to help the situation in any way I can."

Lieutenant Grattan became more incensed when some Cheyenne Indians ran off with a herd of cattle. The cattle traders followed the thieves but retreated when the Indians showed hostility. He was further angered when a Miniconjou "High Forehead" killed a lame Mormon cow which had bolted into a

Brule camp. The Indians regarded stray animals as fair game. The Mormons had reported the incident to the post commander when they had arrived at Fort Laramie. Lieutenant Grattan urged 2nd Lieutenant Fleming who was now in charge of the fort since Commander Garnett had left to let him capture the guilty Indian. They argued long and loud over the problem but finally Lieutenant Grattan won out and was allowed to take charge of the situation.

Peter told Caroline that Caleb had warned him that going into the Indian camp could bring the soldiers a lot of problems. Peter saw Lieutenant Grattan in the sutler's store the day after he took command of the men and arms. He warned him. "Caleb has advised me against such a move. He knows the Indians and says it is better to let this cow go and let the chief punish his own braves.

Grattan roughly pushed him aside and declared, "We have been too soft on them. The only way to stop this is to go in and punish them. I'm taking two 12 lb. field howitzers, one small mountain howitzer and plenty of ammunition. We will blow the red devils to hell. I have alerted the soldiers minding the cattle on the government farm twelve miles away and twenty-nine others have volunteered to go with me. Auguste Lucien, the interpreter is coming too. He did not want to go for the Sioux do not like him even though he has a Sioux wife but he is coming anyway. Wish me well Pete. I tell you it is the only way to treat these savages. Hugh has assigned you and Ned to hold down the fort until we return."

The next morning Peter and Caroline were awakened by the bugle and the noisy sounds of preparations for the departure of Grattan and his detachment. All the men had been drinking the night before and had fortified themselves with a big swig of whiskey just before departure. Peter and Ned both looked with trepidation on the foray and wished that Grattan was not such a brash and determined soldier. They feared for the lives of all the men they had known since coming here and for the new recruits.

In the first four years that Peter had been here the commander of Fort Laramie had changed four times and the fort had been downgraded. Peter was unhappy at the many changes but had adjusted to each new commander and was regarded as a good army man doing his duties around the fort. With Caroline to support him he found the post bearable. Peter had liked Lieutenant Grattan at first but when he saw him shaking his fist at the Indians and cursing them he had told him, "John, you must remember this was their land first and they resent the white man's intrusion."

"Pete," Grattan said, "You must remember we were sent out here to chastise them for their misdeeds and we have been too easy on them. The only good Indian is a dead Indian. Look how they live in their filthy lodges. They are getting more insolent each day."

He seemed friendly with "The Bear" the Sioux chief but he had threatened the other Indians that pushed into the sutler's store.

Harrassments of trains kept on and incidents of Indians brandishing guns and demanding coffee and sugar increased. Since most western army posts were understaffed the emigration of 1854 was greatly reduced. Caroline missed the sight of many trains coming to the fort and meeting the women from the east with news of her home there. Then Brigadier General W. S. Clark of the Jefferson Barracks, Missouri ordered two of the cavalry units from Fort Laramie. Caroline was hoping that Peter might go with them but more of the infantry left. Lieutenant Garnett was transferred and 2nd Lieutenant Hugh Fleming was left in charge.

As Lieutenant Grattan and his men left Peter said to Caroline as he dressed, "They've only got Springfield rifles, Caroline and the Indians have some rifles plus their bows and arrows. I hope they know what they're doing. John is determined to get the thief and Man-Afraid-Of-Horses has advised him not to do it."

The clatter of horse's hooves and the shouting of men and the rattling of the wagons awakened the whole fort and the remaining soldiers and civilians watched as they rode off up the Oregon-California Trail along the Platte.

The group stopped at the American Fur Building and then Lieutenant Grattan commanded them to stop and load their muskets and fix their bayonets. There August Lucien, the interpreter, got another bottle of whiskey to quench his fear at the outcome of this expedition. They continued on past the Oglala lodges and two miles beyond the Brule village Grattan put the gunners through a drill. He was dissatisfied with one soldier's performance and took his place.

They moved on to James Bordeau's place and stopped again. Grattan called out for Bordeau. Lucien fortified with new courage spurred his horse and threatened the Sioux who did not trust the Frenchman and despised him. Bordeau told Grattan that Lucien would only make trouble for them. Grattan asked him to speak with the Miniconjou but he did not want to become involved in a dangerous foray.

Grattan asked to see the Bear, the chief of the Sioux with whom he had been friendly at the fort. Bordeau sent a rider to get Chief Bear. Grattan asked him to try to get the Miniconjou to give up the culprit. The Bear said, "The thieves will not give themselves up. Do not go into the camp." The Bear then tried to parley with Grattan and Lucien.

Since the Indians had learned to give their enemies no

quarter for they had found in their war with other tribes that capture meant certain torture and death they felt that if they gave themselves up it would mean death for them. It was against both individual Indian practice and one of the tribe. They had learned to fear the reprisal of the army which they at first had been led to believe had come to protect them. The Indians in their nomadic life had learned to take what they could to meet the needs of their people. The soldiers were used to making arrests and then finding out the circumstances of the crime.

There was now much confusion in both the Sioux and army positions. When Grattan said, "How, how", to the Indians the soldiers thought he said, "Now, Now," and as the troops leveled their rifles and fired they killed an Indian. The Miniconjous fired back with guns and bows and arrows. The army gunners clipped the tops of the lodge poles with howitzer fire. The Brule were taking their women and children out of the camp. Several hundred braves stripped for war and hid with their horses under a bluff. At Grattan's order the troops fired and the Bear who was retreating fell wounded. Grattan then ordered the gunners to fire again and took his place by the mountain howitzer. The Brule warriors surrounding the soldiers let lose with a shower of arrows. Grattan and four of his men fell before the barrage. With empty guns the soldiers sought to escape. Some jumped on the wagon with one driving. They tried to save three wounded men and the Sioux killed the fourth.

From their position on the bluff hundreds of Brules arose from their hiding place and rode down on the detachment of soldiers. Lucien who was hated by the Indians tried to ride away but he was stopped. They shot his horse out from under him and then though he begged for his life a brave struck him with a tomahawk and killed him with one blow. The wagon with the soldiers made it almost back to the road when a group of Brule warriors killed the men aboard. Man Afraid of His Horse pleaded with the Oglala who were standing in place obeying Grattan's order to save the soldiers but they did not move. He then rode among the Brule and exchanged angry words with them but could not dismay their fury at the army.

The traders were panic-stricken at the melee and barricaded their posts. Bordeaux ran for his gun and ordered all his employees to load all the weapons in camp and prepare for a siege. The civilian who had accompanied the detachment from the fort to Bordeauxs mounted his horse to ride back and notify the fort. The Oglala and Brule were gathering around Bordeaux and charging the building. The whites ran inside as the Indians threatened to wipe them all out. Antone Reynaude, an assistant to Bordeaux and an experienced Indian trader on the Platte, tried to stop them and wrestled with one Indian. A friendly Indian with a rifle tried to shoot the angry Indian but Reynaud knocked the barrel so the charge hit the ceiling and pushed his assailant out the door and bolted it. Some of the warriors wanted to go to the Fort and attack it and kill the soldiers and burn the fort down.

Chief Little Thunder came in and Bordeaux begged him to stop the attack and the Great Father would forgive them. Darkness was coming on and with Little Thunder's intervention along with other chiefs the outraged Indians calmed down and demanded provisions because their children were hungry and they had not received their annuities. Bordeaux opened his storehouse and handed out supplies and Little Thunder spent the night convincing the braves to stop now and not go on to the fort.

Only one soldier had escaped the massacre, Private John Cuddy, who was brought to Bordeaux by a friendly Indian. The Brule warned Bordeaux that if he protected the soldier they would kill all the whites. One of the chiefs suggested to Bordeaux that he hide the soldier in the bushes. Bordeaux asked the man if he could walk to the fort which was eight miles away. Bravely Private Cuddy said he thought he could if someone could go with him. Bordeaux got a Frenchman and two friendly Indians to accompany him and after a mile Cuddy thought he could go on alone. An hour later Bordeaux sent a messenger down the dark road to notify Fort Laramie of the tragedy.

All that night Bordeaux and his men kept on the alert for further Indian retaliation. The Brule squaws had been striking their lodges and moving north across the North Platte. By the dawn they had moved everything taking the wounded Bear with them. About five hundred braves came back to the battlefield to see how many soldiers were killed. They mutilated and robbed the bodies and shot hundreds of arrows into them. Twenty-four arrows had entered Grattan's body and only his pocket watch revealed who he was.

Once again the Brule came back to Bordeaux to demand more goods. They threatened to do to the American Fur Company's warehouse to get their annuities. But according to the '51 treaty they could not receive them after the slaughter of the soldiers the night before. Now both the Brule and Oglala demanded their annuities and a key to the warehouse. The clerk with the key escaped out another door but the Sioux broke in and took the goods.

The Indians had just left when Private Cuddy returned. He had been too weak to make it to the fort. An Indian cautioned Bordeaux that until the braves had gone back across the Platte the soldier should remain hidden in the bushes. Wounded and in severe pain the private hid until all the Indians had gone. Then Antoine Reynaud felt sorry for him and hid him in his blacksmith shop. The next day Bordeaux sent him to the fort in a buggy but it broke down going to the fort. A white trader then took him on his horse to the fort where he died the same day of his wounds.

That same morning the American Fur Company post was besieged by about two hundred Brule wanting more goods. When they were attacking a brother of the Bear came with a message from the wounded chief saying that he had always been friendly to the whites and the American Fur Company was always fair with him so he cautioned his warriors to not break into the store but to leave the post. But it was of no avail for the words of the chief went unheeded and the Indians attacked the door with their tomahawks. The latch gave way and they rushed through and seized all the goods on the shelves. They spilled coffee, flour and sugar over the floor and on the ground outside in their haste to steal the supplies. Then they rode their horses splashing across the river carrying their booty with them.

The day before a Bordeaux rider had reached Fort Laramie. He reported the tragedy to Lieutenant Fleming and warned that the Indians were threatening to burn the fort. Most of the troops at the fort were working outside and Ned and Peter were appalled to hear of the massacre. Not only had Lieutenant Grattan lived and worked with many of the soldiers but the utter miscalculations he had made about the Indians made them wonder if there would ever be peace between the white men and their enemies. This was no way to solve the problem brought on by the white man's intrusion into land originally owned by the tribes of the plains.

Fleming knew that with the hundreds of Sioux on the rampage and his few men that they depended on the goodwill of friendly redmen. If the Sioux struck all the new buildings would have to be evacuated and a stand made in the old adobe trader's fort. Fleming called his ten men together and decided to send a message to Bordeaux to try and make the best terms with the Indians he could. He also asked him to recover the bodies of the dead soldiers. Then he sent a message to the eastern headquarters of the army saying that the Indians were hostile and thinking of attacking the fort and that they needed more troops as soon as possible. A rider was sent hurriedly to Fort Leavenworth to report the massacre where he arrived on September 2, 1854.

In the meantime the Sioux had finally left the region but their depradations were not over. The Brule went north to the Black Hills but they stopped to destroy the government farm that was twelve miles from Fort Laramie and ruin the buildings and implements. On the Niobra River, Chief Bear died from the wounds he had received several days before.

When the Indians had gone Bordeaux buried all the soldiers except Lieutenant Grattan on the field of battle. His body was brought back to Fort Laramie and later buried at Fort

Leavenworth. The graves were so shallowly dug that a Mormon wagon train passed by a month later and some of the heads were visible.

Now all the posts around began preparing for further Indian attacks. The American Fur Post which had been pillaged was barricaded for protection. Some of the traders arrived at the Fort for safety and some went to live with the Cheyenne Indians.

Peter and Ned feared for the safety of Caroline and Iris and Little Ned and Mary Ellen. They instructed them to hurry to the old adobe fort if there were any signs of Indian attack and not to go outside the fort. Caroline felt great concern for the wives and girlfriends and mothers of all the men who had been killed in the massacre. She wondered how a government run by men who did not understand the situation here could handle this new problem. She feared the aroused Indians could not be held back by the handful of men at the fort. She feared for all those who were travelling west and the occupants of the forts along this way. This was a time of desperate worry for all the people in the fort.

Peter and Ned went out with a detachment of soldiers to recover the two howitzers and the wagon. Still anxious about the situation Commander Fleming asked the Indian agent to stop the selling of guns and ammunition to the Indians. The men who had been assigned to out-fort duty were called back and a small blockhouse built among the outer buildings to keep them from being burned.

The officers assigned to inspection duty in the army arrived with Colonel William Hoffman to make an assessment of the situation here. Tensions mounted at the little Fort on the Laramie. Peter and Ned were troubled at the position of the army. They agreed with Colonel Hoffman that Lieutenant Grattan had been a brash, offensive soldier. He had shown his dislike for Indians by kicking aside an old Indian in the sutler's store. He had not understood the Indian character and although he had seemed to like Chief Bear he had been responsible for his death. Many things had led to the tragedy but like many soldiers Peter and Ned had to deal with the problem brought on by unusual circumstances and tragedy.

Caroline realizing Peter's dilemma and the dangerous conditions that had ensued from the Grattan foray had tried to do everything she could to relieve his anxiety. When he came back to their quarters she provided a quiet, restful atmosphere in a sea of conflicting problems.

A warm fire, a pot of coffee, a loving greeting as he wearily trudged in and threw off his army coat after a day of dealing with all kinds of frustrations, were her contributions to his ability to endure the situation at the fort.

Bright Star had left for the day and her help had kept the

quarters neat and clean. Caroline filled Peter's pipe and lit it and said, "Come dear and relax and have a cup of hot coffee. You can only do your best. You must not feel responsible for what is not in your power to change. We can only pray that things will improve and the two sides will come to see the other's point of view."

In each other's arms they would find the courage and strength to meet the rise of a new day on the Laramie.

Iris whose normally happy and complacent personality was able to take most things in stride now became anxious and worried for the safety of Little Ned and Mary Ellen. She said to Caroline in the middle of September, "We can't leave the fort, take rides up the trail, go berry picking or fishing or skating on the river. It really has limited our recreation. I hope things will calm down and we can get back to normal. Bright Star says Long Lance is furious at the death of the Bear and he and other braves want to attack the fort."

"Oh, no." said Caroline. Even with Commander Hoffman and the extra men here we are only protected by such a small force and Peter says their guns are old and ammunition is not that plentiful. Word of the massacre has spread across the prairies and the other tribes are joining in war plans. I hope the government realizes the peril of the settlers there and all the western posts. Maybe the outcrys of all the people will make the government act quickly.

Iris said, "They should do something soon. Every white man west of Kansas is planning on an Indian uprising. Many have been killed already.

Caroline replied. "To think that Colonel Mitchell and the others at the Grand Council were so elated at the signing of the treaty and now all seems forgotten. She took Little Ned by the hand and she and Iris who was wheeling Mary Ellen in a little wooden cart went to the sutler's store where the soldiers and civilians were all talking about the Grattan massacre and what the government and the Indians could do.

Caroline said, "This is one winter when I wish I was home with my family but I can't leave Peter."

Iris answered. "My folks have been dying to see Little Ned and Mary Ellen but Ned says it is more dangerous to travel now than to stay in the fort."

Colonel Hoffman had taken a tour of the fort and asked for a report from Lieutenant Fleming. He asked that the army send a detachment out to punish the Sioux for he feared that all of them would join to slaughter the whites. The officer got first-hand accounts of the affair and he wrote, "We must teach these barbarians a lesson and troops are needed to reinforce Fort Laramie and a strong detachment sent up the Missouri in the spring. Bordeaux and the other traders blamed the Indians and said they had fired the first shot and had been planning to destroy the soldiers.

Many stories were told about the massacre and who was to blame and with the telling new dimensions were added. Peter and Ned were worried about the safety of their wives and discussed with them the seriousness of the situation but both of them were determined to stay where they were.

The army had responded by sending two companies of infantry out in October to add to the garrison at the fort. The commander of the group was Brevet Lieutenant Colonel William Hoffman, a former commander of Fort Atkinson on the Arkansas, an experienced Indian fighter and one who had advocated keeping strength in the western forts. They had arrived at Laramie on November 12 and Lieutenant Fleming was then relieved of his command and requested for another report. In this report Fleming said Grattan had exceeded his orders. Colonel Hoffman after conferring with the other officers decided that the Indians had not initiated the massacre but that Grattan was anxious for a fight. His decision was dismissed by some of the army brass who were trying to absolve the army of any blame in the massacre.

Now the issue became public and Caroline's mother and father heard of the trouble and were worried about Caroline and Peter. Caroline's father had been ill and Harry and Jed were now running his store. They wrote adding their pleas to those of Peter's father asking Peter and Caroline to come home as soon as possible.

Chapter 8

General Harney's Campaign

After the Grattan massacre feelings on both sides were aroused. The Indians, Brule and Miniconjou Sioux were planning for war by collecting arms both guns and bows and arrows. The Platte Indian agent on reaching Fort Laramie found the Arapaho and Cheyennes waiting there for the annuities. Their demands had increased and they wanted emigration over the trail stopped. The Cheyennes were on the warpath too.

At the fort since the Grattan massacre all preparations had been made to resist any Indian attack as long as the men could hold out in their positions. All the soldiers had been recalled from work duty and reports of Indian war parties had kept all the officers and men on alert. Peter and Ned could only hope that with winter approaching the Indians would retreat to their winter camp and that by spring things would calm down. They dreaded the summer of 1855 when more wagon trains would be making their way west and coming by the fort. Colonel Hoffman had tried to make a reasonable assessment of the Grattan massacre but the inflamed eastern citizens were calling for direct action against the redmen.

Iris whose normally happy and complacent personality was able to take most things in stride now became anxious and worried for the safety of Little Ned and Mary Ellen. She said to Caroline in the middle of September, "We can't go berry picking or fishing or skating on the river. It really has limited our recreation. I hope things will calm down and we can go back to a more normal way of living. Bright Star says Long Lance is furious at the death the the Bear and he and the other braves want to attack the fort."

"Oh, no." said Caroline. Even with Commander Hoffman and the extra men here we are only protected by such a small force and Peter says their guns are old and the ammunition is not that plentiful. Word of the massacre has spread across the prairies and the other tribes are joining the war plans I hope the government realizes the peril of the settlers there and all the western posts. Maybe the outcrys of all the people will make the government act quickly."

Iris said, "They should do something soon. Every white man west of Kansas is planning on an Indian uprising and is preparing for such a possibility. Many have been killed already."

Caroline replied, "To think Colonel Mitchell and the others at the Grand Council were so elated at the signing of the treaty and now all seems forgotten. She took Little Ned by the hand and she and Iris, wheeling Mary Ellen in a little wooden cart went to the sutler's store where the soldiers and civilians were all talking about the Grattan massacre and what the government and the Indians would do.

Caroline said, "This is one winter when I wish I was home with my family but I can't leave Peter."

Iris answered, "My folks have been dying to see Little Ned and Mary Ellen but Ned says it is more dangerous to travel now than to stay in the fort for Indian war parties have been harassing the trail."

Since Peter and Caroline had come to Fort Laramie they had met many interesting visitors to the post. In the fall of 1854 Peter told Caroline, "Dear, we have another distinguished visitor coming, Sir George Gore of Sliego, Ireland. He is going to make his base at Fort Laramie and is going to hunt in Colorado."

We had seen people from Europe and the British Isles brought here by the persuasion of Mormon Missionaries to join the members of their faith already in Utah. Last year the Forgren company of Danish Mormons came through." Caroline said. "We have met all kinds of travelers here at Fort Laramie."

"He is very well-to-do and wants to hire Jim Bridger as a guide." Peter said. "He has outfitted himself at St. Louis. He wants to explore the Yellowstone Basin next spring. He will be here all winter."

"Jim Bridger is spending the winter here too so they can get acquainted and make plans for the spring expedition." Caroline said. Mr. Bridger would be a good guide into that country because he has traveled all over and knows the Indians so well since he has had a Flathead, Shoshone and Ute wife." For such a remote post we are getting an education in meeting so many different people."

Sir George Gore came and fascinated the people at the fort with his Irish brogue. He and Ned who came from a town not far from his home made friends at once and they had many interesting talks about Ireland and how things were there now. Sir George was forty-three years old, of medium height with a bald head and short side whiskers, a typical Irish gentleman.

In the spring of 1855, Sir George and Jim Bridger and a big entourage left Fort Laramie. Their equipment consisted of four six-mule wagons, two three-yoke ox wagons, twenty-one French carts painted red drawn by forty or more employees, one hundred and twelve horses, twelve yoke of oxen, three milk cows and fourteen dogs. Peter and Ned, Caroline, Iris, Little Ned and Bright Star watched as the caravan went out the fort's gate.

Ned laughingly said, "Well Sir George is really going in great style. He's taking a wagon to haul his seventy-five rifles, twelve or fifteen shotguns, a large number of famous pistols, two vehicles for fishing tackle and a skilled fly maker to tie flies to catch the fish. One wagon will make a comfortable bedroom when cranked up on the four corners. In addition he has a linen tent 10 ft. by 12 ft. with a striped lining and a brass bedstead that can be taken apart and packed in a small space, a portable iron table and washstand and even a good telescope mounted on a tripod and all kinds of fancy food. Trust the Irish to do things in style. Begorra if I ain't one myself."

Peter said. "Out in that vast difficult region he will need all the comfort he can get. He's a good walker but not a great horseman or shot at a running target. Let's hope they have no Indian attacks or meet up with wild animals. His attendant does all the loading of guns and Sir George likes to break camp early and move at his leisure."

Bridger and Sir George traveled north and hunted the headwaters of the Powder River that summer. After dinner Sir George would invite Bridger to his tent to have a glass of wine and then read to him sometimes from Shakespeare. Bridger said this was "a leetle high faluting for him and he'd be doggoned if he swallowed everything Baron Munchawson said," and he thought "he was a durn liar. He himself could tell stories about his travels with the Blackfeet that would be marvelous if they went down in a book."

The party drifted down the main valley of the Yellowstone River. On the Tongue River they "forted" for winter. One of the men accidentally started a brush fire and all the stock had to be moved so Gore and a few of the party took care of them. Sir George had a small log cabin built and he spent the winter with his favorite horse, a grey Kentucky thoroughbred. They fed the other horses cottonwood bark like the Indians but his horse ate cornmeal. The Blackfeet on a hunting party discovered them and wanted to steal their horses but were run off by the men. The Piegans were more successful and ran off with twenty-one head. The third tribe to try to take horses, the Bloods were discovered before they made off with them and one of the Indians was killed.

One man in the party died and Sir George dismantled a wagon box for a casket. The usual burial in the mountains was in a blanket or buffalo robe and a shallow bier with a pile of rocks to mark the grave but here too Sir George did the right thing and had a proper burial.

Early in the spring of 1856 Sir George went up the Tongue River, crossed over to the Rosebud Valley where they met a village of Crows. They traded for some horses and Sir George returned to his winter camp to have two flatboats built to carry part of his trophies down to Fort Union. While there Major Alfred J. Vaughn the Indian agent for the upper Missouri and Alex Culbertson visited him while taking the Absarokas their annuities. Vaughn took a dislike to Sir George and wrote a caustic report the following July to the Superintendent in St. Louis. He disliked Sir George's hunting and trading with the

Crows and his sport of killing bear, buffalo, elk and deer. His report was exaggerated but he said that Sir George had killed many bears, buffalo, elk, deer, antelope and small game. After the flatboat had floated to Fort Union, Sir George went by land and hunted along the way. He arranged for the effects to go down the river on the fur boat and contracted with Culbertson for a mackinaw boat to carry the rest. He offered to sell his surplus goods but didn't like Culbertson's offer so he had the rest burned and threw the refuse into the Missouri River. He went down to Fort Berthold and spent the next winter and then returned east and home to Ireland.

Peter and Ned had learned of this trip when Bridger returned to Fort Laramie and they told Caroline and Iris that this was one Irish gentleman they would not soon forget.

The Oglala seemed more peaceable and contacted Colonel Hoffman but the Brule were furious when their chief, Running Bear died. They threatened to kill all the whites on the trail that winter and meet the troops in the spring. On November 13, 1854 the mail wagon going west was attacked by the Brule and three men were killed and $10,000 in gold stolen. Incidents of Indian depredations spread across the prairies to Missouri frightening the Indian agents who joined with the army to ask for punishment for the tribes. The Hunkpapa, Sans Arc, Blackfeet and Yanktons joined in the uprisings. The outcrys forced the government under President Franklin Pierce to set aside appropriate funds to send an expedition against them. In October, 1854 the Chief of Staff of the U.S. Army Winfield Scott had decided that Brevet Brigadier General William C. Harney should lead the army expedition to settle the Indian problems in the west. He was a fearless soldier, and experienced Indian fighter from the battles against the Seminoles in Florida and Wisconsin and a man of action and swift retaliation. In his army career he had taken decisive action against the British in a dispute over the San Juan Islands in Puget Sound and the battle of Cerro Gordo in the Mexican War. Now he was given the task of subduing the Plains Indians. Scott's call came on Christmas Eve and Harney did not hesitate, like a dedicated soldier he left his family and met President Pierce at the White House who told him to "whip the Indians at all costs."

Word arrived at Fort Laramie that General Harney was to head the expeditions and while Peter regarded him as a great officer, he wondered just how with his reputation for impetuous actions he could help the strained relations between the army and the Indians around Fort Laramie.

General Harney quickly arranged for troops and supplies for his expedition. By early June he was on his way to Fort Leavenworth. There he took command of seven hundred cavalry, infantry and light artillery soldiers. Colonel Phillip St. George

Cooke was to accompany him on the trip. Cooke had led the Mormon Battalion from Santa Fe to California in the Mexican War and so he had had experience with both the Indians and the west. He would be a valuable assistant to General Harney on the trip.

This was the biggest army expedition ever marshalled against the Indians. General Harney wanted to challenge them at the beginning of winter giving them a hard choice of deserting their families or starving.

Peter returned to their quarters after Colonel Hoffman had held a meeting with his officers informing them that a rider had come from Fort Leavenworth to tell the fort that General Harney was coming with a big detachment of soldiers to punish the Indians for their attack on Lieutenant Grattan and his men.'

"He said to Caroline who was cooking a big pot of stew over the fire. "Darling, Colonel Hoffman says that the chief of staff Winfield Scott is sending Brigadier General Harney west with the biggest force ever sent against the Indians."

She asked, "But Peter isn't it late in the season to be attacking the Indians?"

"He thinks," Peter said as he took off his uniform and put on his robe, "that he will punish the Indians at the time of year when they have to fight or desert their families and leave them to starve."

"What a cruel choice," Caroline said. Bright Star is very unhappy that Long Lance and her brothers have ridden north and west to get the Cheyenne and Blackfeet to join in a war against us but she can't help but feel sympathy for her people." But Peter we can only do all we can to help a difficult situation. Come and try some of this venison stew. Caleb brought me a nice piece of venison and Iris had some vegetables to add to it. I've made some saleratus biscuits in the dutch oven."

"Darling," Peter said as he kissed her. "You give me hope when all is topsy turvy around me and bring calm to an impossible situation. We can only hope that General Harney has the wisdom to see both sides of the problem and not make it worse."

"Only time will tell," Caroline said. Meanwhile let us be happy together and not let this unhappy situation spoil our relationship or our love."

"Never," said Peter. "I knew when I first saw you that you were the only girl that I could every love and I am more convinced of it now than the first night we spent together. General Harney will leave in early August to come west. We must be prepared to help him in any way we can. At this time of year there will be little grass to feed the cattle and horses and mules he will bring with him. It will be a difficult trip for the men and animals."

121

Peter and Ned began making preparation for the arrival of such a force space in the barracks would have to be doubled and many would have to spend the cold Wyoming days in tents. Even the officers would have to share quarters. They hoped it would not take long for the Indian problem to be solved. In August the oncoming soldiers would not realize how cold the winds were in Wyoming Territory or what the campaign would require of them.

On August 10th Peter had been introduced to Thomas Twiss the new Indian agent who came from New York and was an older man with a white beard. Peter liked him immediately and respected his concern for the Indians. He believed in the superiority of the whites and regarded the Indians as poor helpless children. Twiss met with the Oglala at a post north of the fort and followed with a parley with the Washasha band advising them to be friendly with the whites. September came with most of the Sioux some four hundred lodges concentrated south of the North Platte on the upper Laramie River. The Brule and some of the Miniconjou who had participated in the Grattan massacre were staying farther north in the Black Hills. Swiss sent word to Harney that he had separated the good Indians from the bad.

Little Thunder a wise and peace-seeking chief had been trying to keep the braves under control but some small bands were attacking posts along the Platte and stealing their horses. One Brule band those how had attacked the mail party, among them Red Leaf brother of Chief Bear and Spotted Tail his cousin had been the Grattan attackers. Long Lance had accompanied them on some of their forays against the whites. Everytime he had visited the fort Bright Star had begged him to quit attacking the whites for she had heard that General Harney and a big expedition was coming to punish the Indians and she feared for his safety knowing his impetuous nature and his hatred for the soldiers.

The Indians had learned that the expedition was coming and a runner for the Indians at Laramie Fork arrived to warn them and invite them to come to a council at Bordeaus. The hunters had just killed buffalo and would not move. General Harney was receiving information about the Indians and knew that 40 lodges or about 400 people were on Bluewater Creek a tributary of the North Platte. Some of the braves had been insolent to emigrants near Ash Hollow and kicked over a coffee pot. Harney sent a messenger to Little Thunder asking for a parley. He said they could have peace as well but if not the soldiers would fight.

On September 2, General Harney crossed the North Platte. Little Thunder sent word that he wanted to parley. Harney ignored the chief and decided to attack. The army camped at the mouth of Ash Hollow and General Harney sent scouts out to the bluffs to reconnoiter. In his tent he gathered his officers and told them of his plans. Cooke with the cavalry would start at three in the morning and go south around the Indian village and station themselves behind the camp. General Harney with the infantry would attack them from the front crushing them between the two forces.

Cooke was ready and the men were saddled up at the appointed hour. He led his men through the quicksands of the north Platte ten miles around the Brule camp. His men dismounted and tethered their horses and lay in the grass with rifles ready looking down on the sleeping village.

General Harney waited to see if Cooke was in place and finally sent a scout to see if the cavalry was on the bluffs. He came back with no assurance that Cooke and his men were there so General Harney was undecided about their approach. Little Thunder rode out with his braves and asked for a parley but Harney kept marching and refused to talk to them.

The Indians who were now worried about the situation and raced back to their village. The squaws had struck most of the lodges and some of the Indians were moving on horseback up the Bluewater when the soldiers arrived.

When Harney was not sure of Cooke's position because an aide had said that the ground was too hard for Cooke's men to reach their assigned position, Harney decided to wait and parley until he was sure Cooke was ready to attack. He sent an interpreter to propose a talk.

Little Thunder said if the troops would halt he would meet them to talk. Harney agreed and both sides paused and Little Thunder had asked a second time for a parley and came out with a white flag but other witnesses said that Harney initiated the parley to gain time to see where the cavalry were located.

Little Thunder rode up and was invited by Harney to dismount. He was attired in colorful regalia and was wearing the medals bestowed by his white friends at the council of 1851. He was worried now about the fate of his people. He offered Harney his hand and the General refused. Little Thunder tried to be conciliatory but Harney finally exploded with, "We have come here to fight."

Little Thunder pleaded with Harney to let his people go but Harney said, "You must fight. I have not come out here for nothing."

Little Thunder pleaded with Harney again not to attack his people but Harney paid no heed to his plea.

Just then a squaw and two Indian children crossing the stream saw Cooke's forces on the ridge. She ran back to warn the other Indians. Two young warriors challenged Cooke's men to fight and Cooke withheld his fire because he had not heard the guns of the infantry. The whole Sioux encampment now knew of the trap set for them and scattered in every direction. Many climbing the embankments that had small caves and brush for concealment. General Harney now knew that Cooke had reached his place on the hill.

He ordered Little Thunder to tell his warriors that they must fight. The chief mounted his pony and raced back to his people. The infantry began firing as the bugler sounded a charge. The forward company poured a devastating fire into the fleeing Indians as they plunged into the Bluewater to attack those climbing the embankments.

At the sound of the first infantry shot, Cooke and his men mounted their horses and trotted in as a column of fours across the Bluewater to head off the fleeing Indians. On the way Cooke sent a company downstream to stop those who tried to escape by crossing the canyon to the east. Then with his main force he charged the Indians who had climbed to the top of the eastern mesa. The Sioux dropped back from the cliff under a withering fire and some were able to catch their horses at the bottom of the ravine and ride off east across the river but only the fastest, youngest braves were able to escape the surrounding soldiers. Many were hurt and unable to carry their wounded with them in their haste to escape the trap that General Harney's men had planned for them.

In mid-morning the general gave orders for a recall. The cavalry was still pursuing the Indians over the prairies. Some of the soldiers had stopped shooting to aid the wounded. Many women and children had been killed and the soldiers suddenly realized the enormity of their deed. One officer when questioned fifty years later could not describe the scene of carnage. Some of the men and the army surgeon assisted the wounded back to Fort Laramie. Eighty-six Indians had been killed in the foray. More could have been carried away as the warriors carried their dying with them. Bloodstained trails marked the path of their retreat. Seventy women and children were taken captive. Only four soldiers were killed, one missing and seven wounded. In rain the women and children were taken back to Fort Laramie.

General Harney felt his mission had been a triumph and reported proudly that "The results were all he had hoped for." Much later he came to see the futility of such an action. Even some of the civilians at Fort Laramie who were afraid of the Indians were jubilant over their flight.

Peter and Caroline and even Ned for all his experience and bravado were sickened by the pitiful sight of Indian women and children who were herded back into the fort. They were moaning in grief and misery and a rain storm made the scene even worse. Cold and wet, losing loved ones and their homes with winter coming on, they were desolate. Later they were moved to Fort Kearney.

For the next two days the troops looted the Indian camp of

robes, saddles and powder horns. Everything they thought valuable they carried away. The drying buffalo meat was used as the soldier's main food for a day. Here they found the papers stolen in the murder of the Salt Lake mail employee as well as bayonets, and pieces of uniforms taken from Grattan's dead soldiers. What goods they did not want were burned. They left the remains of the dead on the battlefield as one soldier said, "we left the bodies to the wolves."

In exultation after his victory Harney had his men erect an earthwork fortification near the mouth of Ash Hollow which he called, "Fort Grattan." He then marched on to Fort Laramie on September 9 and left a company of infantry to protect the Oregon trail.

The Indians in retaliation attacked three white men below Scott's Bluff and mortally wounded one. Then on September 15 a few warriors came into the stockade as if to trade and while the herdsmen were lounging in the shade by the walls they drove off about fifty of the fort's horses and mules that were grazing outside the fort. When Harney arrived at the fort he sent a large detachment in pursuit but they could not apprehend the thieves. He burst into profane language when apprised of their lack of success.

The Harney campaign had not produced the effect on the Indians that the government had hoped for when he was sent west. It had only created more trouble for the Platte Indians had named him "the Wasp" and the young warriors were more determined than ever to get even with the white men. Colonel Hoffman, the commander of Fort Laramie, had rightly assessed the Grattan massacre and the Harney expedition. He warned his officers to be on the alert for Indian reprisals against the fort and took action to make it safer.

Peter and Caroline and Ned were sickened by the stories about the massacre and the sight of Indian women and children who were herded back into an unused building at the fort. It was now getting very cold and uncomfortable for them. Ned helped find shelter for them and brought food from the commissary but such things could not assuage their grief or their bitterness against the soldiers.

Bright Star went to see her aunt who had two small children and had seen her husband killed at Ash Hollow. She came back sobbing to tell Caroline, "Soldiers kill our people and take them prisoners. Why? Cannot we both learn to live together?"

Caroline put her arm around the Indian girl and explained, "It is the government who doesn't understand your problems. The soldiers are doing what the officers order them to do, they have no choice but some of them are more vicious than others."

Bright Star could not be comforted and she soon went back to her lodge outside the fort. She worried for fear Long Lance had been one of the warriors who had driven off the fort's horses and mules and she feared that the soldiers would try to recover their lost animals and that once again her people would be killed.

Now that autumn was here General Harney began to worry about continuing his campaign in winter. He talked to Colonel Hoffman at Fort Laramie and discovered that Lieutenant Grattan had forced his way into the Indian camp and with a drunken interpreter had precipitated the massacre of the soldiers many of whom had been drinking. General Harney did not drink but was tolerant of his men if it did not interfere with their duty. He now was reassessing his report to the army on the need to punish the Indians.

Peter came back to their quarters and told Caroline that General Harney now had a broader view of the Grattan affair. The post chaplain had said that Grattan himself was intoxicated and that the soldiers were drunk. The General sent a detachment down the trail to break up Fort Grattan an earthwork fortification built near the mouth of Ash Hollow.

On September 29 General Harney and his column who had bivouacked outside the fort left Fort Laramie and crossed the North Platte river. The officers at the fort were not sorry to see him go though they respected his position in the army and his former army career. They were feeling the cold night temperature and the effects of a chilling rain. The night temperatures were often below freezing as they moved up the old trader's road towards Ft. Pierre.

Caroline told Peter as she put another blanket on their bed, "I feel so sorry for General Harney's men. It is getting very cold in the mountains and already we have felt the cold here. It was raining all night. They must be miserable in camp. Sometimes I get so angry at the army and the commanders."

Peter replied, "There are good and bad men in the army just as in any civilian job. They are only doing their duty as they see it. Sometimes they go too far. Colonel Hoffman is very reasonable and understanding of the Indian's plight and realizes that young inexperienced officers can make serious mistakes. One tragedy only leads to another."

Caroline said, "Oh Peter, I will be glad when you are relieved of your duty here and we can go back home. Even though I loved all our friends here I can't help but be worried by the tragic things that have happened."

Although the General and his men were now in Indian country the scouts had not seen a single Indian. The Sioux had retreated to the Black Hills after the massacre. They were avoiding any further contact with "The Wasp" as they had named General Harney. His guides had advised him against invading the Black Hills because of the danger to both he and his men and animals at this time of year. He had decided to go on to Fort Pierre which had become an army base.

They lost only one man as the column reached its destination on October 19th. The fort was not the warm well-kept post they had hoped to reach. It was in a delapidated condition and the cold Dakota winter made it miserable. The army cattle succumbed to exposure and lack of food. Over a third of their horses died and others were frostbitten on their ears and tails. The lack of vegetables brought scurvy to the men and some died.

Before early November 25th the Miniconjous visited the fort and pleaded with General Harney to have peace with them and let them live. They returned some of the horses stolen at Fort Laramie and a boy who was said to be the one who killed a Mr. Gibson on the Oregon Trail. The boy escaped fearing reprisals when camped nearby and all the Miniconjous disappeared. Then forty Sioux from various tribes visited the General a few days later and said they were poor and in want and asked only to live in peace.

General Harney was now sure that it was the right time for a peace council. He met the Sioux representative on November 9th and gave them the copies of a paper asking for the men from each tribe to a peace council at Fort Pierre on March 1, 1856. Although the snow was deep and the temperatures freezing whole tribes came to the fort. At midday on March 1 they joined with Harney and his staff in a meeting in front of the stockade. Little Thunder, Harney's old enemy, was there but the Oglala were not present. Thomas Twiss their agent did not agree with Harney and advised them to stay away. Harney was so furious he ordered Colonel Hoffman at Fort Laramie to arrest Twiss and to send a delegation of Oglala to the council. Twiss was relieved of his duties and later had to go to Washington to get himself reinstated.

At the Fort Pierre meeting as in the meeting with Little Thunder at Ash Hollow Harney refused to shake hands. The Indians quietly made a circle on the cold ground and the general outlined his demands. The Indians were to stay away from the trails, give up the culprits who had harassed the emigrants and return stolen property, quit fighting each other and to give up trying to pay the traders for the murder of whites by gifts of buffalo robes. He threatened, "Otherwise we will have blood for blood."

For these considerations the United States Government would protect the Sioux from white intrusion, would allow the Indians to take white offenders to the nearest post, to restore their annuities and to set free all prisoners not guilty of a serious crime. The General concluded the meeting asking that they think over his offer. The next afternoon Little Thunder and the Sioux returned saying that they did not wish to fight and that he wished to shake hands with the General.

Harney responded that if they would meet his conditions that he would shake the chief's hand. Harney arranged to release the Brule women and children captured at the Ash Hollow massacre.

The Indians agreed to give up the men who had killed Gibson and the Mormon cow. For three more days they talked. Harney gave Little Thunder official paper making him the principal chief of the Brule. Then he extended his hand to him. With their applause, Harney gave commissions to all the chiefs and subchiefs and shook hands with them. To close the council he gave his soldier's blessing to the redmen saying, "I hope the Great Spirit will take care of you and that he will put good in your hearts and that you may have plenty and keep your heads and hearts clean that you may not be afraid to meet the Great Spirit thereafter." With tremendous applause the council ended and the next day two thousand Sioux came to the fort to salute the General with drums and horns.

In his message to the Secretary of War Jefferson Davis, Harney pleaded for the United States Government to work to gain the confidence of the Indians and bring peace. Davis recommended that President Pierce make the agreement valid.

The Indians moved quickly to confirm their contract. In April the officials arrived at Fort Pierre from Fort Laramie. Commander Hoffman had followed General Harney's instructions and arrested Thomas Twiss their Indian agent. Peter and Ned reluctantly agreed with his decision but were sorry that it was necessary. They felt that Twiss had the Indian's interests at heart. By May 15 the Miniconjou had surrendered High Forehead who had killed the stray Mormon cow. Harney had been ordered to close the Sioux campaign and return to Fort Leavenworth and release the prisoners captured at Ash Hollow.

Two years of tragedy had been the result of misunderstandings and miscalculations. As Thomas Hart Benton, Senator from Missouri said, "It is a heavy penalty for a nation to pay for a lame runaway cow and for the folly of a West Point fledgling."

Peter told Caroline when reading the Benton remarks, "Grattan was a brash inexperienced fellow. We who are from West Point are not all so ready to destroy the Indians. Some of us can understand their feelings and see the problems of communication between our two races. Since Colonel George W. Maypenny had been sent three years ago to visit the border tribes and urge them to sell their lands there has been a big rush west to Iowa and Nebraska by settlers. Colonel Maypenny is one of the most honest men appointed as an Indian agent and interested in their welfare. The treaties led to the sale of thirteen million acres of ground for farming. Many of the flood of new landowners stole the Indian's property, destroyed their timber and mistreated them."

Caroline said, "How can the Indians trust the white men. Didn't Colonel Maypenny make good treaties?"

Yes, Peter said. "but unscrupulous white men used money and liquor to gain their ends. The Indians have retaliated by attacking surveying and road building crews and the army does not have the troops to protect all of them.

Caroline replied, "Yes and despite the Grattan and Harney massacres the Sioux still make Fort Laramie their headquarters. Bright Star does not seem to be blaming the soldiers here even though General Harney killed her uncle and some of her other relatives. I wonder if there will every be a time of peace between us. You have been here almost seven years Peter and there seems to be no end to the constant struggles and more and more settlers are coming from the east to take up land now all along the trail. When I came out the farms and ranches were far apart and great stretches were open country."

Peter said, "Well we have served many emigrants coming west and I hope we had some influence in keeping the problems reduced. No Indian tribes will ever be happy at the loss of their lands and food."

Chapter 9

A Year Goes By

Peter was unhappy at the results of General Harney's campaign for he felt that the General's actions had only caused further trouble between the Indians and the army at the fort. He feared for Caroline's safety and for awhile he wanted to send her back to her parents until he could join her at a post in the east. She refused saying that she had not come out here to be a part-time wife. She was going to stay despite the danger.

Peter saw the killing of Little Bear as a tragedy for he had known him well and considered him to be a conciliatory chief and one who had cautioned his young warriors against hasty actions and had been a friend to the white man. He saw only future problems for the men at the garrison on the Laramie and more attacks on emigrants coming west.

Later two white men from Fort Pierre came into Fort Laramie after walking twenty-four miles from Rawhide Creek. The Sioux had struck once again. Another party of emigrants had camped on the Laramie River and the Indians had stolen all their mules even though the emigrants had shot at them.

Peter and Caroline once more were disturbed by the news and the report that General Harney wanted to kill every Indian he could. The Sioux were naming him "The Wasp" and said they had felt his sting. Peter and Ned were keeping on the alert for an attack on the fort. Guards were posted every day and night and carefully checked to see that they were on duty.

It was hard to reconcile the differences in culture between the Indians and the whites. To the Indians any stray animal was fair game. The army insisted on assuring the property rights of the emigrants, teamsters and other travelers on the trail. It was a constant battle between these two points of view. In the first four years of 1849 to 1853 their fort's commanders had been changed four times and none of them had had time to adjust to the problems there. Only Peter and Ned and a few privates remained of the soldiers who had come in 1849. Their disciplined deportment kept the fort as safe as it was despite conflicting problems.

The winter of 1854-55 was a long one for Peter and Caroline and the temperature dropped to frigid degrees. General Harney had planned to move his troops north to Fort Pierre to spend the winter. Colonel Hoffman had convinced him while he was there that Lieutenant Grattan was a brash, headstrong young man and that the Grattan massacre was the result of misunderstandings and abrupt action of the troops. Caroline was glad when his troops moved away from Fort Laramie for his presence only further provoked the Indians. His men had not stayed inside the fort for there was no accommodations for them there but had bivouacked outside. Caroline and Iris and the children were not allowed to go outside the fort and their skating expeditions were stopped. They still visited at the hotel when music and a dance was planned and enjoyed associating with their friends at the fort. One of the other wives who had visited in the summer had gone home saying the "Boredom here was too much for her." Caroline was glad that an Indian attack did not change her mind.

One night as Peter and Caroline lay in their big wooden bed he pulled her close to him and said. "Dear, if we don't snuggle close we will be cold before morning. I could not stay here if it was not for your sweet presence."

"Oh sweetheart," Caroline replied, "I wish the army would call you to some other post. It is so hard to see our friends both Indian and white in such a turmoil. Bright Star's uncle and other relatives were killed at Ash Hollow. Only her father Roaring Bear was saved when he hid in the bushes on the hill. He is very angry now and wants revenge and before he was one of the friendly Miniconjous who asked for a parley and peace. Bright Star can see no hope of an end to the hostility."

"I am needed here now," Peter said, "if only to urge some reason on the men who want to destroy the Indians. We have really stirred up a hornet's nest by killing so many of them."

"Can anyone ever find an answer fair to both the white man and the Indians? Caroline asked. She reached for his hand but he had gone to sleep tired from meeting the problems of the fort and his frustrations at dealing with the more belligerent officers.

Caroline felt sorry for the laundresses who worked so hard over scrub boards and tubs to keep some sort of clean clothes for the army. She had made friends with Maren a little Danish girl who had come to America to find that alone she would have to support herself in the only way she could. The older girls, Helga, Karen, Rose and Jane had been with the army at Fort Leavenworth before coming to Fort Laramie and knew all the sorry conditions they would face. Rose was now Sergeant Dick's girl and they were planning to be married as soon as the army chaplain could marry them. Rose was beginning to show signs of pregnancy beneath the full calico dress she wore. She was an English girl a cockney born in the slums of London and she knew all the foibles of life there as well as in America. At socials at the sutler's store the laundresses like the soldiers were often drunk. Life at the fort was not conducive to good conduct among its occupants. All of the vices of a frontier fort were evident in the violent carousing that regularly took place. Sheltered and apart from the general melee Caroline still realized the forces that made otherwise rational men indulge in momentary pleasure. Loneliness and disgust with both Indian hostility and government pressure played a part.

Caroline had run out to see what she could do for the helpless Indians victims of this last army attack when they were brought into the fort. Peter asked her to go back to their quarters.

"Why do they do this Pete?" Caroline asked. "Don't they see how terrified it is for these innocent women and children. Why should they pay for the misdeeds of the young braves?"

Peter only shook his head. Trained to believe in the actions of the federal government and under army discipline, he still had no reasonable answer for their actions. He had sent letters to the officers he knew at Fort Leavenworth trying to urge some reasonable solution but many congressmen and officers in the Department of the Army little understood or really cared about problems in the west and had forced this more desperate action.

Winter was coming to the fort. The bitter cold weather had forced the soldiers on guard duty to wear heavy buffalo robes over their uniforms. It was hard to tell which were army men and which Indians or civilians. The cold wind that swept the Laramie plain made the officer's quarters and barracks hard to heat. One fireplace for each quarter provided heat that was uneven and inadequate. Caroline found that one blanket was enough at the first of the night but before morning one or a buffalo robe was needed on top.

The fort was not comfortable even in the spring as one of the visiting wives had said, "When the wind blows off the snow one does not see sprouting grass but only barren sand."

Arrivals and departures of people at the fort were major events and interesting people found their way into the hospitality of the post. Everyone stopped their duties just to see who was coming and going. A never-ending stream of emigrants made a stop at this last camping spot before going into the mountains and crossing the divide.

Caroline had become most friendly with Maren among all the laundresses. The little Danish girl had large blue eyes brightening her face and making her fair skin and long blonde hair really beautiful.

"It is too bad," Caroline told Peter, "that Maren does not have someone here to look after her. The other girls are well able to look after themselves."

Private Carr is very taken with her but so are half of the enlisted men," Peter answered.

"I only hope," Caroline said, "that she finds a good man who will be kind to her. She has no one in Denmark now. Her mother died and her father has remarried."

In a few weeks a happy surprise took place. Peter told Caroline that Private Carr had asked Maren to marry him and they would be married in May at the chaplains. Caroline broke the good news to Iris and Ned and the two couples and Mr. and

Mrs. Bullock gave a reception at the hotel for them. All the fort's citizens of any consequence were invited and it was a gala occasion. Caroline had made a ruffled, lace-trimmed white dress for Maren and she looked beautiful with her long blonde hair, blue eyes and pink and white complexion. Private Carr was in uniform, his dark hair brushed until it shone, his uniform newly laundered and starched to a stiff elegance and his boots spit polished to a mirror gloss.

Even a few friendly Indians came to gape at the couple and partake of the fruit punch livened by a generous addition of whiskey. Some of the guests ended up the evening by becoming intoxicated and causing the provost marshal to remove them from the premises but most enjoyed the occasion to the cutting of Iris's huge fruitcake and best wishes to the bride and groom. Everyone left with small samples of the cake to be put under their pillow. The newlyweds were to spend the night at the hotel. Late into the night the sounds of banging pans and horns could be heard as Private Carr's friends held a chivaree for the couple. Private Carr had been ordered back to Fort Leavenworth and had been made a corporal so they were taking a coach east the next morning.

Caroline said sadly as she pulled on her flannel nightgown and brushed her long dark hair, "I hate to see Maren go. She has been a good friend to me."

Peter agreed, "And Private Carr has been such a help at the fort but perhaps we will still see them again when we go east. I hope to get my orders soon to another post."

The expedition of General Harney so praised by the Department of the Army had not put to rest the Indian problem as some of the eastern establishment hoped. The emigrants were still coming in large numbers bringing their loaded wagons down the trail and the buffalo were becoming more scarce each year. Some of the hungry Indian women were coming to the fort to beg for food. The Indians were feeling the pinch of hunger now for their men had to ride far south to find the buffalo that before the coming of the emigrants had been plentiful close to the fort.

Some of the soldiers were restless and looking for trouble to liven their dull lives. In August 1855 word came that Jim Bridger and Louis Basquez his partner had turned over their post to Louis Robison, a Mormon scout sent by Brigham Young. Jim Bridger had spent the winter of 1854-55 at Fort Laramie.

Brigham Young the Mormon leader claimed that as Indian agent he had sent a posse out to take over the post because he claimed that Bridger was selling arms to the Shoshone and the Ute Indians that were used on attacks on the Mormon settlements. Previously in 1853 the Mormons under Orson Hyde had built Fort Supply near Fort Bridger. Feelings at Fort Laramie were mixed some people siding with Jim Bridger and others with the Mormons.

Even though there was tension between the soldiers and the Indians there were good times too. The soldiers were given a day pass for fishing, hunting and gathering berries. Variety shows were performed on the balcony of "Old Bedlam" The Laramie Minstrels, a musical group entertained at fort functions.

One day in the summer of 1855 when things were calmer and Peter and Ned had a day pass Caroline and Iris organized a berry picking and picnic excursion. Bright Star went along to help with Little Ned and the baby. Service berries and choke cherries were plentiful along the river and Bright Star knew where the best bushes could be found.

"My mother dried many berries," she said, "to make puddings in winter. The berries are plentiful under this moon."

They set out early in the day with Peter on Diamond and Caroline on a small black and brown horse called Brownie, Ned riding on his big sorrel mare, carrying Mary Ellen. Iris holding Little Ned in front of her on a gentle brown mare and Bright Star riding her pinto Indian pony. They carried several baskets to hold the berries and a lunch that Caroline and Iris had prepared. Some of the soldiers called out to them as they left the fort, "Get some for me, and Ned replied, "We'll give you some jelly."

They traveled down along the river where Bright Star said the service berries were plentiful. Peter and Ned dismounted and helped Little Ned down to look at the river and came back to tell Iris, "You'll have to watch the boy for the water is deep in the pools along the side."

Caroline said, "I'll help to watch him too. We'll take turns picking berries."

"My mother once picked berries every summer." said Bright Star. "My mother who is with the Great Spirit for many moons. My father enjoyed her puddings. They could see that Bright Star was still grieving for those of her family who were killed by General Harney.

Iris said, "I've been making service berry jam every since I came to the fort. There are not many fresh fruits out here. At home we had strawberries, apples, pears and peaches. We canned a lot of fruit for winter and made big jars of jam."

"They can be dried," Bright Star said. "Our women use them in many ways."

Peter and Ned had brought their fishing poles and were finding a good spot to throw in their worms. "Come on fellows," Iris called. "Help us with the berries and then you can go fishing." Reluctantly the two men came up the bank and took the baskets. They soon had a basket of the purple berries and Caroline and Bright Star had filled theirs. Iris took Little Ned's hand and they went down closer to the river and then returned to the picnic spot where the baby was sleeping soundly on a blanket.

Caroline said, "Let me watch him for awhile Iris and you can help fill the other basket." She played with Little Ned rolling his big red ball to him and having him throw it back.

"Why don't you fish for awhile and then we'll have lunch," Caroline said.

"Suits me fine," said Peter, "but I can't wait for a piece of your dried apple pie."

The men soon returned with a string of trout apiece and cleaned them along the bank. "We're going to have a great fish dinner tonight." Ned said. "It will be a good change from the bully beef and beans that the commissary serves."

Iris and Caroline with Bright Star helping set the tin plates and knives and forks on the red checkered tablecloth and laid out the lunch. They were hungry now and everything tasted good in this outdoor setting.

Iris said, "It is so nice not to have to worry about Indian attacks like we did last year."

Caroline said, "We were virtual prisoners in the fort but I am glad they did not attack. They are so many while our men are so few."

Ned said, "It is not over yet and the Indians have many grievances they have not settled."

"Here in this beautiful setting," Peter said. "It is hard to imagine that such tragedies could happen. We must always be on the alert though for the troubles are not over."

After lunch Caroline and Peter rested on a blanket under a willow tree by the stream while Bright Star watched the baby as she slept and Ned took Iris and Little Ned down where they could sit on the bank and fish in a deep pool. Soon they heard Little Ned squealing and he came racing back to Bright Star with a trout dangling on a forked stick.

"Look what my pa caught," he yelled. Iris ran after him to make sure he got back to the picnic spot safely. "We have enough fish now for a good dinner." she said.

"Isn't it lovely here Peter," Caroline said. "I could stay here for a long time it is so peaceful and cool and listen to the river."

"Darling," he said as he kissed her. "These special times are worth all the times of worry and stress at the fort. I wish we could suspend time and just be here forever."

They were interrupted by Ned who came by to say that they had caught enough fish and it was time to return to the fort. They caught the horses which were hobbled and grazing nearby and soon were on their way back to the fort.

Life went on as usual at the fort. A few emigrants were coming into the fort now but as the autumn days shortened most of them would decide to stay on there at Laramie instead of trying to cross the mountains when the snow was beginning to whiten Laramie Peak. Peter performed his duties each day and the Commander praised him for his help and attention to duty. One day he came back after seeing the soldiers marching on the parade ground and Caroline said, "Dear, you have been a great influence for moderation and understanding on both sides. So many people can only see their own point of view. They have been lucky to have you as an officer at Fort Laramie." "And you, my darling, have been so dear and understanding." Peter said as he kissed her. "Very few wives have been such a help to their husbands here. The day I came down with Charles to meet you was the greatest day of my life."

"It is mutual," said Caroline, hugging him tightly around the waist. "No circumstances can ever change my feelings for you. You just can't get rid of me," she joked.

The Commander has recommended me for promotion as a captain." Peter said. "I am hoping we can go back to a base near home. Your Pa and mine haven't been so well the past year and it would be a big help if we could be closer to home."

"We can only hope that you will receive your commission soon. As much as I want to go back east I will still miss the fort and our friends, Ned, Iris and Little Ned and the baby, Caleb, Bright Star and Mr. and Mrs. Bullock. Life has been so exciting here with its many problems and meeting so many different kinds of people. The west has opened up and the country will never be the same again. Nothing will stop the number of settlers coming out here. The lure of gold, freedom and new opportunities will bring more and more of them to the west," Caroline replied.

Peter had been promoted from second lieutenant to first lieutenant since he had been here and had been recommended for advance in rank to Captain by the commander of the fort. The eastern army command was slow in responding to the wishes of many of the western fort officers and many of them were reluctant to confront the problems of such remote posts and some considered them unnecessary to the interests of the eastern establishment and only sources of trouble with the Indians. More enlightened congressmen and government officials wanted to see the west settled and the United States expanded to the Pacific coast.

Peter dressed and said to Caroline in one morning he was free to spend as he pleased, "Dear after breakfast I am going over to the stables and see how Diamond is doing. I really came to appreciate that big black horse when I had to come out here with Major Sanderson. He carried me over every rocky trail and rough terrain without a fall. Do you have a carrot or a lump of sugar I could take him?"

"Surely dear," Caroline answered and went to the cupboard

to get them for Peter.

She sat down and was knitting on a shawl for Iris's birthday and mused Peter has matured and grown more understanding. He is heavier now, more sure of his position in the fort and not as ready to make hasty decisions. He is firm with new recruits but ever ready to hear their personal problems and try to solve them.

Peter leaned down and kissed her and said, "I'll be back from the stable soon. Now that things have settled down maybe we could take a ride tomorrow if it is a good day. I could tell the stable boy to have Diamond and Brownie ready for us."

He crossed the parade ground waving to Ned as he made his way to the stable. "Hello Sergeant, nice day for a picnic. I'll see you later.

Private Hersh had learned of his mother's death in the east from the chaplain and being bored and unhappy at the fort had decided to steal Peter's horse Diamond and desert the post. Peter heard Diamond whinnying and snorting as he approached the stable. The private had tried to saddle him but the big black horse who was getting heavier and objected to a strange rider had moved restlessly in his stall. Just as he was trying to tighten the cinch, Peter confronted the private.

He shouted, "What are you doing there Private Hersh? That's my horse."

Diamond was trying to nip at the young soldier with his teeth.

Private Hersh stopped and wheeled around. "Lieutenant, I only wanted to take a ride," he said. I am so damned sick of this god forsaken place I can't stand it. My mother just died in Pennsylvania and I want to go home."

Peter grabbed the young recruit by his collar and shook him.

"Soldier, you know the penalty for desertion," he said. "They will hunt you down and bring you back and you will be chained to the cannon as punishment. Not only that but the Sioux are watching the trails for lone riders and you could be scalped and killed. They would show you no mercy. I realize the problems you have here but we are all under great stress here. We joined the army to protect our country and the hardships we have had here are only a part of our job. I am sorry about your mother but I know she would not want you to desert your duty."

The young soldier was sobbing now as he dropped down on a stool in the stable.

"Buck up, Peter said. "I know it is a lonely post and not a great place to be. I have my own dear wife Caroline to support and comfort me and without her I would be desolate here but there are things to do. Do you play an instrument. They need musicians in the band and there is a library here and the Chaplain will talk to you. Go to him and tell him your troubles."

The young man straightened up and said, "Lieutenant, you

won't report me then."

"Not this time but only one reprieve soldier. Do not try it again. Besides Diamond could buck you off. He doesn't like strange riders. Peter went to the big black horse who had been restlessly pawing the ground and patted him on the head and gave him the carrot and sugar. Then he threw some more wild hay into the feed box. "Good old boy," he said and patted him once again on the head.

"Go back to your barracks, soldier and come and talk to me tomorrow," Peter told the young man.

The soldier said, "Thank you Lieutenant. I shall not forget this." and ran out the stable door.

Peter stayed to brush Diamond down and to talk soothingly to the big black gelding.

"Old boy," he said. "We have been together a long time. I am glad I discovered Private Hersh in time or I hate to think what could of happened to both of you out on that lonely trail."

He went back to their quarters to tell Caroline what had happened. She agreed with him that he had made the right decision. Private Hersh had been a model recruit until now and only unusual circumstance had made him want to desert.

Chapter 10

Goodbye to Fort Laramie

The spring of 1856 came to Wyoming Territory. There were still many unresolved problems for the two combatants in this war between the redmen and the whites. Both felt they had been ill treated and there was still a big group of easterners who wanted to move west and take up Indian lands. Some of the Indian agents like Thomas Fitzpatrick, Thomas Twiss and Colonel George Maypenny had been understanding of Indian problems and even though Maypenny had gone west to get the tribes to sell their land he had advised the government to live up to their promises. Too many others had corrupted the plains Indians with bad liquor, disease and unfulfilled promises.

Thousands of new emigrants were coming west to settle in Indian land and in Kansas and Nebraska. Some mistreated the Indians and stole their property, timber and possessions. The Indians responded by attacking surveying crews and road building laborers. The cavalry had to accompany the workers. In April a detachment of troops with Peter and Ned accompanying them were sent out to guard the Platte Bridge near Caspar, Wyoming. The commander seized three Cheyenne for an offense of harassing the men. In response the Cheyenne killed a trapper who was going to Fort Laramie and then harassed the trail near Fort Kearney.

Caroline and Iris and Little Ned who was now four years old waited fearfully for their husbands and father to return from the trip. The Grattan massacre and the Harney reprisal against the Indians had left lasting scars on their consciousness and every movement of the soldiers was awaited with dismay by the occupants of Fort Laramie. They had experienced the turbulent years of Indian and U.S. Army confrontation and were now realizing how dangerous the life in a western frontier fort was. As spring came on the stream of emigrant trains from the east going to the Mormon settlement in the Great Salt Lake Valley, the opening of Oregon Territory and the gold fields of California kept the Fort a place of constant change. Caroline especially liked to talk to the young girls her own age and ask them about the east, the conditions of the trail and just why and where they were going.

Some of the trains like the Donner party which had met tragedy in the Sierra mountains in 1846 seemed ill prepared for the trip and had to dispose of many of their possessions at Fort Laramie before they could go on into the mountains. Caroline and Peter purchased a little organ from Mr. Bullock that a train member had found too heavy for the trip over the South Pass. Caroline had Peter and Ned and Private Carter carry it to their new quarters and she spent many hours practicing on it and entertaining her friends and Peter with the music when they were visiting.

All kinds of goods were left lying on the trail around Fort Laramie as train captains advised by Caleb and other mountain men and guides to lighten their loads before entering the mountains disposed of their excess baggage. Their oxen and mules were already trailworn and exhausted, suffering from shoulder sores and lack of food when they reached the fort. Many wagons were repaired at the blacksmith shop and others were discarded. Peter was constantly answering questions about the road west and conditions there.

Caroline felt the Mormon trains were usually well equipped, well planned and ready for the trails ahead. The members were industrious, well motivated and had a good understanding of the possible dangers. Still only the experience of traveling over the Rockies could really give them a knowledge of the problems they could face.

Both Peter and Caroline had learned to love many of the people at the Fort. The post chaplain had been very kind to them, inviting them to services and advising them on meeting the problems of frontier life. Bright Star had been such a help to them. She was a hard-working cheerful and beautiful Indian girl. One of the privates had made advances to her but she had long loved her Indian friend, Long Lance a brave in the Oglala tribe and wanted to marry him. He was often out on hunting and war parties. Bright Star longed to see him more often. She liked the people of the fort but was loyal to her tribe. She hoped that Long Lance could learn to like the white people but so far he resented bitterly the attempt to take his land, kill the buffalo and bring disease and whiskey to his people. He did not trust the Long Knives for they under General Harney, had killed his father at Ash Hollow. He had only escaped by hiding in some brush and then catching his horse and riding across the river to the east. He had joined the other young warriors in raids against the immigrant trains and fur posts.

Caleb too had befriended them and his advice about the Indians and their problems had helped Peter to understand just how to advise the other officers at the fort. So many of the army men had come out to the fort determined to annihilate the "savages" as they called them. Peter had earned commendation for his balanced view and efforts to bring peace to an unhappy situation. Both the soldiers and the Indians respected his sense of fairness and ability to stop the potentially dangerous fights inside the fort. All the commanders had appreciated his work and later Peter and Caroline learned in April 1857 that he was to be promoted to Captain and assigned to a post in the east. Caroline was delighted with the recognition Peter had now received. For

140

too long both had been chafing at the incompetent men sent to take charge of the fort, the frequent change of commanders, the lack at times of sufficient soldiers and up-to-date arms to man the fort and the attitude toward the Indians that many had. Peter would go back to Fort Leavenworth to receive his new commission and then be assigned to a new post. Caroline would accompany him to Kansas and then go on home to visit her parents while Peter traveled to his new assignment. She would join him there as soon as she could.

They hated to leave Ned and Iris and Little Ned and Mary Ellen. They had become fast friends and had helped to make the life here more pleasant for both Peter and Caroline.

Caroline hoped that Long Lance would soon settle down and marry Bright Star for the little Indian girl was ready to have a lodge and children of her own. He had been gone for several weeks now to the south on the Republican River to hunt for buffalo which had become scarce in the Black Hills. Before he had gone he had ridden up to the fort to see Bright Star and then dismounted to talk with her.

"Your uncle will accept my offer for you of two horses and a buffalo hide," he told her. "I am going south with the other braves to get the buffalo. Word comes that many have been seen in the hills there after the last full moon."

He was dressed in buckskin hunting clothes and was riding a pinto pony. He was a handsome brave, Caroline thought as she saw them together. His long hair was held back with a colorful beaded band. His jacket and pants trimmed with quills and fringe. Bright Star too was colorfully clad in a leather jacket and skirt she had made and decorated with elaborate beadwork and was glowing with excitement and joy at her lover's visit.

"Come back soon," she whispered to him. "My uncle Running Antelope will be waiting to welcome us."

Bright Star had learned to speak English by working at the fort.

"You will wait for me," he ordered fiercely. "You must be my squaw. Long Lance must have you." His dark eyes flashed with anger.

"The Wakonda or Great Spirit be with you and may you have a successful hunt." Bright Star answered. "I will wait for you." Maybe the tam-do-ka the buck and ta-to-ka the big horned antelope will be there too."

He jumped quickly on his pony and was gone out the gate of the fort and Caroline put her arm about her shoulders.

"He will be back" she said. "Come and help me with my packing. Peter and I must leave in two days for Fort Leavenworth and I must get my things ready.

"Sorry friends go," Bright Star said. "Good friends to Indian people. Many Long Knives cheat and hate my people and give them firewater. You are different. I wish Long Lance could see you as I do."

"Yes," said Caroline. "We have many friends here. Peter is a very fair and kind man. I am proud of him."

"Wish all Long Knives like Peter." Bright Star said. "He understands how we feel."

"Someday," said Caroline, "Both sides will understand each other. Then they will live side by side in peace."

"Many moons will pass before this comes," Bright Star predicted, "and there will be killing and the ground will once again be bloodied. Only then will they learn to understand each other."

Iris came then to see if she could help Caroline. Little Ned with his bright brown eyes and shock of red hair was hopping along beside her. She was pushing little Mary Ellen in a makeshift cart that Ned had made.

Caroline went to the door to welcome her. "Hello, Iris," she greeted her. Bright Star is helping me to get my things packed. "Come in Little Ned" she welcomed him as she patted him on the head. "Let me hold Mary Ellen awhile. I am going to miss you all dreadfully."

Iris said, "We will miss you too. We are happy that Peter got his promotion but we are not looking forward to the fort without you. Ned does not know when he will be called to another assignment. I hope it won't be too long but the Indians troubles are not over and he has had experience with them. A lot of sergeants coming out are new to the west. They need a few men who understand the Indian problems out here. Bright Star after you help Caroline here would you come over and help me wash some diapers, Mary Ellen can use a big pile in a hurry."

Bright Star answered, "I am glad to help both friends."

"Did I see Long Lance ride out of the fort." Iris asked.

"Yes," Bright Star said. "He is going hunting for buffalo then he come for me."

Meantime Caroline was cuddling little Mary Ellen, holding her tightly against her heart, feeling the soft warmth of a sleeping baby, her dark head against the blanket, singing softly as she rocked.

"I hope you and Peter can soon have a baby of our own," Iris said. "When you get settled again at your new post."

"Me too, Caroline said. "We both want one so bad. They are so dear and sweet. Mary Ellen is a darling and Little Ned is the dearest little boy. He reminds me of little Jed and Harry, my nephews. They must be quite big now it has been six years since I have seen them. I will be glad to see all of them again. I didn't know that it would be that long when I came out here. My father hasn't been well and I am so anxious to get home."

"I can understand," Iris said. "My parents live in

Connecticut on a farm and I will be so happy to get home once more. Ned's folks are in Ireland and he doesn't hear from them often. His mother and father died last year."

"Peter will miss all his friends here," Caroline said. "Mr. and Mrs. Bullock have been so kind to all of us. The sutler's store has been a big help to the emigrants who need new supplies."

"Can I pack some of your clothes?" Iris asked.

"Most of them will go in this big portmanteau," Caroline replied.

Iris neatly folded Caroline's dresses and skirts and blouses and laid them carefully in the big bag. Caroline laid Mary Ellen so gently down on the bed that the sleeping baby did not stir. Iris told Little Ned to go outside and play with his ball.

"I'll put Peter's uniforms in," Caroline said. "Some of his clothes are at the laundry. Ingrid said they would be ready later today."

He always looks so neat and well-dressed." Iris said. "Ned doesn't take such good care of his clothes but then sometimes he has duty on the hay or wood detail and he comes back with lots of thistle in his trousers and sawdust in his hair. Fort Laramie sometimes is a dirty place when the wind blows the sand about."

"Yes, Bright Star is continually sweeping out the dirt that sifts into our quarters." Caroline replied. "When the snow goes there is lots of sand around. I'll miss our skating parties on the Laramie River and the parties at the hotel and sutler's store. Mr. and Mrs. Bullock have always shown us such southern hospitality and they have such lovely Victorian furniture in their parlor that it made me think of our parlor at home."

"The stage is due in Friday," Caroline said, "and we have to be ready to go at noon. Peter says it should not be too bad a trip to Fort Leavenworth at this time of year. He still does not know where he will go after that. We are hoping it is in the east or at West Point where we can visit with our folks often. Peter's father has been writing asking us to come to see him. Peter is his only child and after his mother died they were very close."

They had finished packing and putting their books into a separate bag.

"Here is a Bible the chaplain gave us," Caroline said. "We will always be grateful for the interest he has shown in us and all the men at the fort. We have really met some interesting people here, mountain men like Jim Bridger with all his tall stories to tell. Thomas Fitzpatrick, the Running Bear, the Oglala chief who was killed at Ash Hollow, James Bordeaux, the first trader at Fort Laramie for the American Fur Company before the army came, Man-Afraid-of-Horses, a Sioux chief, Lieutenant Grattan and General Harney. There has been so much turmoil and change right here. The gold rush was at its peak when Peter came. The many Mormon emigrants who were going to their Zion in Utah.

They all passed by and many came up to the Fort. Peter and I have taken part in the opening of the west and the settling of the stops along the Oregon Trail. It has been an exciting time even though we have had many dangers to face."

Iris said, "Ned, that old red-headed Irishman of mine has been right there with Peter. I'm sure they will never forget each other. I must get back and take little Ned for his nap and feed Mary Ellen. We'll see you at the party tomorrow night. Bright Star," she said to the Indian girl, "are you through here?"

Caroline dropped the things she was packing and said as she accompanied her friends to the door. "Mr. and Mrs. Bulloch are having a farewell party for us tomorrow night at the sutler's store. We hope everyone of our friends can come."

"We wouldn't miss it for anything," Iris answered. "Bright Star had offered to stay with the children while we come. Goodbye for now."

Peter was finishing up his work at the fort. The commander had called him in for a farewell talk and to ask his advice about problems he saw ahead. While some of the Indian chiefs wanted peace the young braves like Long Lance were still causing trouble along the trail. The resentment of the Indians could not be stilled by broken promises and treaties.

The Commander said, "Peter, I heard good reports about your conduct here and how valuable your advice and actions have been while here, I have sent a letter of commendation to Fort Leavenworth and to the Secretary of the army in Washington."

"Thank you sir," Peter replied. "I will miss everyone here."

"Your wife has been an attractive asset to the fort life. She is a very fine woman and beautiful too." the Commander added.

"Thank you sir," Peter replied. "It has made life here much more pleasant to have her with me. It was a great sacrifice for her but she has made the most of it."

The wives who come out here are exceptionally brave," the Commander said. "It is loyalty beyond the usual duties of a wife. I know since my wife left last fall just how lonely and boring this life can be. I hope she can come out in June again. She couldn't bear it in the winter. That is all Lieutenant Meade. Good luck to you. If I see you again which I hope to do you will be Captain Meade. I'm sure in time you will be a colonel and even a general. We need good leaders in the army."

"Thank you sir," Peter responded.

"Oh, said the commander as an afterthought, "I will see you at the party tonight."

"Good," said Peter, "Until then."

Caroline had left one nice dress out of the portmanteau. It was blue with a lace pleated front and a touch of lace on the sleeves. The skirt flared out over her starched underskirts and a bustle at the back added to its charm. It was Peter's favorite dress.

Peter had spit shined his boots, put on a new uniform and brushed his dark hair carefully after he had shaved his dark beard with a straight razor, stropping it on a leather strap.

"My you look beautiful," Peter said to Caroline. I'm glad I'm taking you away or some new officer might fall in love with you."

"Oh, you know better," Caroline said. "I'm glad there aren't many girls here. You look so handsome I would have to watch you every minute."

He kissed her and held her tenderly.

"No one can ever come between us," he assured her. "You are my one and only love."

"Wait until later and I will show you how much you mean to me," he whispered.

The May night was cool and delightful as they walked across the parade ground to the sutler's store which was lit up with kerosene lanterns.

"Here comes Caleb and Waiting Star," Peter said as the mountain man and his squaw came into sight. "I'm glad they could come. He is one friend who really knows the west and the Indians and their problems. For all their difference in cultures Waiting Star has been a good wife for him. Jim Bridger had several Indian wives. I wish he could be here. He would have some lively stories to tell tonight, but he has gone east since his fort was taken over by the Mormons.

"Some of our Indian friends are gone now and the government wants to put them all on a reservation," Caroline said. "I hope things work out for them. We will always be unhappy at the things that have been done around here."

"And the sad thing is that both are to blame," Peter said. "The Indians make war on their own people. They should work to help each other. They need it so desperately.

The music of the organ in the Bullock's parlor could be heard now, playing Auld Lang Syne and their conversation was ended as they entered the store. Mr. and Mrs. Bullock with courteous southern hospitality greeted them warmly and invited them to have refreshments and a drink at the long table set up in the store. Mrs. Bulloch was known for her delicious dried apply pie and desserts and the table was laden with all kinds of food.

Second Lieutenant Carl Moody and his wife came in next. They had only been at the fort for a short time and the young officer had just graduated from West Point. Peter had tried to make him a part of the fort's officer corp but he was a stiff arrogant young man. He seemed so sure of himself and his army training that he resented anyone trying to help him and to explain the situation here at Fort Laramie. He regarded the

Indians who hung around the sutler's store as savages and rudely kicked a Sioux who had had too much to drink and was in his way. The Indian had drawn his knife and only Peter's swift intervention had stopped a serious fight.

Instead of appreciating Peter's help he had resented him. His wife was a short white girl with mousy colored hair and nondescript features. She seemed to cling to him and allow him to dominate her completely, a shadow following behind his commanding personality.

He had paid special attention to Caroline to all the dances at the post, asking her to dance with him and avoiding Peter's presence. He admired her beauty, her poise and her friendly way with people.

"You have such lovely eyes," he said as they met in the square dance.

She was used to having the men make complimentary remarks to her for she knew how lonely and bored they were here at the fort with little feminine companionship. She had learned to turn away any romantic overtures with a friendly retort and her obvious love for Peter. Most of the men respected Peter and recognized in Caroline a girl of character and inherent good sense. She tried to be friendly with all of them and if one of them became tipsy and out of control and tried to become too intimate with her, Peter and Ned were always there to protect her.

"Lieutenant, I hear you are leaving soon. How can Fort Laramie get along without you? When will we ignorant easterners know all you have learned about life in the west?"

"Moody, you are learning fast," he said. The Commander will make good use of your help. Everyone is essential in running this post. We have never had enough men or arms. Then to his wife, "Hello, Elizabeth, would you like a drink of punch, someone has spiked it but not too much."

"Caroline," Moody said, "You are looking especially beautiful in that blue dress. Maybe you could give Elizabeth some tips on what clothes to wear."

"Thank you for the compliment," Caroline said. Elizabeth looks very pretty tonight. It was nice of you to come."

"We couldn't miss giving Peter a sendoff," Moody said sarcastically. We know how essential he has been to the fort."

Peter overlooked his sarcasm and saw that he was beginning to slur his words and Elizabeth pulled on his arm and whispered that the music was beginning for another square dance.

The teamster who played the violin was tuning up his instrument and with a harmonica played by a traveler and the jew's harp played by a passing emigrant the music began again. The other guests were coming with several sets of dancers the room was soon twirling to a do si do. Peter and Caroline joined one set with Iris and Ned and the Moodys danced with another. Caroline was surprised to see how graceful Elizabeth Moody was and how the shy girl enjoyed mixing with the other dancers. Carl Moody could not keep her under his domination here.

Caleb and Waiting Star had helped themselves to the food and drink and were sitting on the benches along the wall. Several of Peter and Caroline's Indian friends had joined them and were watching the dancers. The other officers on the post dressed in their uniforms were either dancing or watching. All of them came over and spoke to Peter and Caroline and wished them well at his new assignment.

Carl Moody was glaring at Peter and getting more intoxicated with every drink from his hip flask. Elizabeth kept remonstrating with him but he only brushed her aside. A sergeant asked her to dance and she went to join the dancers in the schottishe.

Moody made his way over to Peter and Caroline who were talking to the Commander and swung Peter around by the shoulder.

"Come on you Indian lover," he yelled. "Let's see who's a better man. Put up your fists." He threw off his uniform jacket and stood defiantly staggering slightly.

Peter, now angry at Moody's belligerent attitude at a time like this started taking off his coat. "Peter, you know he is drunk, please be careful." Caroline protested, "let us make this last evening a pleasant one." Ned had come up then, "Pete, don't let this rascal make you fight."

The Commander had summoned the provost marshal. He was getting tired of having some of the new young recruits making trouble on the base.

Ned said, "Come on let's put him in the guard house to cool off."

Together they led the struggling second lieutenant out of the dance.

Elizabeth Moody was in tears at the episode, "Please forgive him," she begged Peter. "He has had too much to drink. This is his first assignment and he has a lot to learn." She excused herself and ran from the room outside into the night.

Caroline felt sympathy for Elizabeth but decided to overlook the incident as she had done many times before in this volatile place.

"Come on Peter," she coaxed. "Let's finish the dance and get some of Mrs. Bullock's delicious pie."

Peter was glad to put on his jacket and return to the party. Ned came back in a short time and said, "We settled him down for the night. I hope he learns a lesson. There are too many problems out here to be fighting with each other. It's enough to try to find peace with the Indians. Come on Iris let's join the

147

dance."

The party ended after midnight with Peter and Caroline thanking Mr. and Mrs. Bullock for the nice party and their friends for coming. They had only one more night here in this boring post. They could hear the wolves howling outside the fort.

Caroline said, "They are really hitting it up tonight. They must be hungry."

Their little terrier Tipsy started barking as they opened the door. "Come on it's time to go outside a while," Peter ordered. Tipsy had been easily house-trained and had learned to sit up and beg and was a welcome addition to the household.

"Ned and Iris would like to have her. Little Ned loves her. She is so well-trained. I wish we could take her with us but since I don't have an assignment yet it would be hard to find a place for her." Peter said.

"Yes," Caroline replied, "and I couldn't take her to ma's place. Pa is still sick and Muffie our old dog is too feeble to have a younger dog around. That is just another friend we are leaving here at the fort."

Peter brought Tipsy back in and said to Caroline, "Remember the first night you came to me here. It was so wonderful to see you I could hardly stand it. It seems so long ago now and so many things have happened since.

"Yes," Caroline answered as she disrobed, putting her blue dress into the portmanteau. "But we still have each other. I will always come to you no matter where you go if they will let me."

"You are so beautiful and such a sweet lovely girl. You aren't a bit spoiled by all the attention and compliments you get. I was so lucky when your cousin Charles brought me down to meet you."

"Darling," she said, come on to bed. There will never be anyone as sweet and dear as you are. Tipsy please go on your rug," she ordered the dog who had jumped upon the bed. Tipsy obediently hopped down and curled up on the rug by the door.

Together they would find fulfillment in their love. It would obscure the coolness of the Wyoming night, the worries about the future, the unpleasant aspects of the past. They had built a firm relationship of mutual respect and admiration. Together they could meet any problems and resolve them.

About the Author

Frances B. Thorn, the author, was born in East Mill Creek, Salt Lake Country, Utah, a granddaughter of early Utah Pioneers, an alumnus of the University of Utah where she majored in History and English. She has been a life time student of history. She has written biographies of her pioneer ancestors, one being published by the Utah Historical Society in the centennial year of 1976. She is a member of the Daughters of Utah Pioneers and was a former captain of Carrigan camp. She has written one book on the Utah War, *Defend, Defend,* five historical novels, *Saddle Creek, The Desert Trail, Next Stop—Fort Laramie, War in the Rockies,* about Johnston's Army and *They Met Again at Shiloh,* the last three a triology of novels. She has been a wife, a mother, a grandmother and a widow, which encompasses all aspects of a woman's life. She has written many poems, one of which was published, "Thanksgiving Prayer," short stories and a children's book called *Animal Stories by Grandma T.*